Khadafi

Anthony Fields

**Lock Down Publications and Ca$h
Presents**
Khadafi
A Novel by *Anthony Fields*

Khadafi

Lock Down Publications
P.O. Box 944
Stockbridge, Ga 30281

Visit our website @
www.lockdownpublications.com

Lock Down Publications
Like our page on Facebook: Lock Down Publications @
www.facebook.com/lockdownpublications.ldp
Cover design and layout by: **Dynasty Cover Me**
Book interior design by: **Shawn Walker**

Anthony Fields

Stay Connected with Us!

Text **LOCKDOWN** to 22828 to stay up-to-date with
new releases, sneak peaks, contests and more…
Thank you.

Submission Guideline.

Submit the first three chapters of your completed manuscript to ldpsubmissions@gmail.com, subject line: Your book's title. The manuscript must be in a .doc file and sent as an attachment. Document should be in Times New Roman, double spaced and in size 12 font. Also, provide your synopsis and full contact information. If sending multiple submissions, they must each be in a separate email.

Have a story but no way to send it electronically? You can still submit to LDP/Ca$h Presents. Send in the first three chapters, written or typed, of your completed manuscript to:

LDP: Submissions Dept
P.O. Box 944
Stockbridge, Ga 30281

DO NOT send original manuscript. Must be a duplicate.

Provide your synopsis and a cover letter containing your full contact information.

Thanks for considering LDP and Ca$h Presents.

Dedication

This book is dedicated to my son Amari Tariq Fields and both of my parents who gave me life. I also dedicate this book to all the men on death row at Terre Haute Penitentiary.

Acknowledgements

First and fore most I have to say that all praise is due to Allah. Next, I'd like to thank all the people that support me and appreciate what I do. I have to shout out my woman, Lashawn Wilson. When the chips were down you were still around. For fifteen years you existed to hold me down and I appreciate it. To my sisters, Toi and Tonya. I love y' all dearly. I had to let the past go and realize that I really love you two.

Always know that y' all little, big brother is here for y' all. To my brother Woozie. I pray that one day you regain your freedom. Your sons, Asa and Dooley are young men and they carry on the Fields name well. To all my nieces and nephews, I love y' all. To all my extended family members that support me, thank you. To all the good men in the struggle, I'm here. You all know who you are. I been home for a few months now and if I haven't got at you, either, I don't mess with you or I forgot. Real talk. The people that I love and respect, know who I love and respect.

To Nene Capri, thank you for all your help and advice. You told me to start with a fresh pen and I did, thanks for everything. To my man Delmont Player whom is next to blow, I got you, dug. To all the good men in prisons everywhere, shout out to you. To Kenneth Simmons, I love you, Goo.

To Antone White, Angelo Daniels, Colie Long, Trey Manning, Cochise Shakur, Marquee 'Kilo' Venable, Khalif,

Lil Man, Fice and others, keep yall heads up. To Poochie Mason, I love you. My cousins Michelle and Avonda Brown, Cowanna and Donna Marshall. Thanks for the support. To my cousins Herb Austin and Ray Ray, I salute yall. To everybody I didn't name, blame my head and not my heart. One love,

Buckeyfields
    DC Stand up!

Anthony Fields

Chapter One

Beaumont Pen
August 2008

"The white boys sent word that they are gonna kill one of their own in the cage today. I fuck with Richie and the Boston white boys, so they gave me a heads up. So, y' all need to get ready for a lockdown," Ameen announced as he walked up to the cage. "He might be dead down there already."

We were in the fifth cage on the SHU's rec yard. The administration still had Ameen on the three man hold since he copped to the Keith Barnett murder. A couple months after I committed one of the worst murders in the history of the Bureau of Prisons, I was anxious to go home and do exactly what I needed to do. *Kill.* Starting with Lil Cee's family. "Aye, cuz, who they supposed to crush?"

"The dude name Big Country. They said word just came from another yard that he was a rat in the state joint in Nebraska. You know them AB niggas don't play that rat shit."

"Neither do we." Boo blurted out.

"I already know that, ock. You know what I meant."

"Just bullshittin' with you, slim. I'm hip to the white boys, they be punishing their own like shit. For whatever reason, they killing. Ain't no faking with them. Them and the Mexicans shit say work call off the break."

Ameen got down on the ground and did a set of pushups. "Y' all see what them niggas did to lil Gabriel."

"Man, fuck Lil Beast hot ass." I added. "That nigga should've been dead. All the telling he did."

"Who did Beast tell on?" Umar asked.

"The question is, who didn't he tell on?" Ameen replied

as he got up off the ground. "That's why I laughed when I heard about how he sold that Mexican all that death and the Mexican crushed his ass."

"Cuz, no bullshit, the way they did Beast was gangsta. I thought my shit was gangsta. Them niggas slipped their cuffs and stabbed the CO, took his keys and went in Beast cell and killed him. Movie shit all day."

"What you did to Keith still out gangstered their demo."

"Don't look down there but they are butchering the white boy in the last cage right now." Ameen told us.

I tried not to look, but I couldn't help it. I am drawn to violence like bees to honey. I could hear the commotion and the white boy Country's cries. His pleas fell on deaf ears as several other white boys stabbed him repeatedly.

"Everybody on the rec yard, get down on the ground! In every rec cage! That means you, too, Fuller!" The SHU rec officer yelled as he ran past our cage. "Put the weapons on the ground and back away from that man! Do it, now!"

"Fuck we getting on the ground for? Like we can get outta this cage or something." I groaned but got down anyway. We laid on the ground and watched all the correctional staff rush the cage where the white boys were. They rolled a stretcher out to the cage, but by the looks of the white boy that had been stabbed, it was too late for that. What he needed was a coroner. We didn't make it back to our cells until three hours later. I was hungry, tired and mad as shit. I climbed on the top bunk and closed my eyes. "Aye, cuz, wake me up when the food get here."

****

"Aye, slim, the pigs at the door looking for you." My celly Kenneth 'Goo' Simmons said as he tapped my foot.

Sitting up in bed, I glanced at the door as saw a CO staring at me through the glass on the cell door. "What's up?"

"SIS, Fuller. Neal wants to see you. Get dressed."

"Fuck that bitch nigga want with me?" I asked myself as I get off the bunk and slipped my jumpsuit on. "My celly coming with me."

"I don't give a fuck. He can cuff and come along."

"Cuz, go with me to see this SIS nigga. He might be trying to try some slick shit. I want you there with me."

"Say no more," Goo replied and got dressed.

Once we got to the LT. office in the SHU, Lt. Darius Neal looked up and saw me and Goo entering the office. "I called for Luther Fuller. Not Luther Fuller and friends. Why're you here Simmons?"

"He's with me. We're on the buddy system so that none of my words can get misconstrued. That always seems to happen nowadays."

"Carlson leave Simmons out in the hall for a minute. My conversation with you Fuller will be brief." After, Goo was lead out the room, Lt. Neal said, "So, you're just gonna let Felder take the murder beef, huh? While you go home and get killed, huh? That's how your story is gonna end?"

"I don't know what you're talking about. None of it."

"You know exactly what I mean, Fuller. I been around you for years and I know you. I been around dudes like you all my life. I understand how you operate. Did I ever tell you that I have a psychology degree and with a criminal justice degree?"

"Naw, but why should I give a fuck?"

Lt. Neal laughed. "That's the answer that I expected. But I just wanted to talk to you…"

"Don't you got other shit to do besides try and psychoanalyze me? I heard that a muthafucka got killed in the rec cage today. Shouldn't you be somewhere investigating or something? Instead of harassing me?"

"Harassing you? You haven't even seen harassment, Fuller. I ain't gotta harass you, I read all your mail and intercept all your kites. Like I said, I just wanted to look you in the face and see your expression when I asked you what I asked. You and I both know that Antonio Felder didn't kill Keith Barnett and chop his body up. Don't we?"

"I have no clue about anything you're talking about. What did your rats tell you?" I asked.

"Wouldn't you like to know. I just figured you for a stand up kinda dude. You know, like the type that takes his own beef."

"Don't know what you're talking about. Are you done with me? Can I go now?"

"Yea, you can go. You just proved everything I thought about you."

"Oh, yea, and what's that?"

"You just proved to me that you're the type of piece of shit that will do anything to cover his ass and duck being a real man."

I rose from the chair that I sat in. "Like I really give a fuck about what a pig think about me. Fuck you, cuz."

"Yea, fuck you, too, but I got one more question. Why did the white boy get killed outside in the rec cage?"

Without a word, I turned and left the room. I could hear the lieutenant laughing behind me.

Chapter Two

"Then this nigga gon ask me about the white boy situation outside, cuz. Bitch nigga got me all fucked up, like my shit got informer in my jacket. Faggie ass pig." I complained as I paced the cell. "Nigga, talkin' 'bout he know me. That nigga don't know me, cuz. Don't nobody really know me. Somedays I wake up and don't even know myself. There's so much inside of me, cuz. So much shit that has fucked me up. I be hearing voices and shit. Having nightmares and all kinds of shit. I just repress that shit. Keep all that wild shit inside me."

"That's why you lunching like that. For all the above shit you just said. You can't keep that shit bottled up inside you, slim. Bad shit has a way of eating you up from the inside out. Believe me, I know. They charged us with 38 murders on my RICO case. I got found guilty of 5 of 'em. A lot of shit that I did, slim, didn't even have to be done. Senseless shit. I don't even remember why I killed half the muthafuckas that I killed. Now all this time I got be fucking my head up. I know who I am now, but in a few more years when it finally settles in and I accept the fact that I'ma die in here, I'ma be somebody else. A way more dangerous muthafucka."

"I feel you, cuz. No bullshit. My life could be different right now, had I not gotten away with all the shit I did in my past. The only difference between you and me is that I didn't get caught for all the muthafuckas that I killed."

"How many people do you think you killed, slim?" Goo asked.

"Besides Keith's hot ass?"

"Yea, besides him."

I thought about what Goo asked and did a count in my mind. "Shit, cuz, that's a good question. I never really counted them all before."

"Damn, young nigga, you ain't nothing but twenty-six. You haven't been alive long enough to not remember how many people you killed. Do you even remember why you killed so many? Or how old you were when you caught your first body?"

All the stuff that I had done in the past rushed back and played inside my mind with vivid clarity. It was as if I was watching my life story on the Lifetime channel in HD. I remembered exactly how old I was when I killed my first victim.

"I ain't never told nobody my life story, cuz, because nobody never really asked. Like you said, maybe I need to get that shit outta me, so I can stop hearing the voices in my head that tell me to do certain shit. When I say that I hear voices, I'm not talking about no weird ass schizophrenic shit either. There's a beast that lives inside of me. A real animal spirit that only knows one thing. *Killing.* When I heard that Keith Barnett was coming to Beaumont, all I thought about was Mousey and all the shit that he'd told me about his case and about Keith. Then I remembered all the pain and suffering he went through because of betrayal and that shit made me so mad. I remembered the promise that I made to Mousey the day we parted in Atlanta Pen."

"If I ever see that nigga, cuz, anywhere in the system, I'ma smash his ass. You got my word on that."

"I believe you slim and I'd appreciate it. Straight up. That nigga needs a good killing."

"The beast inside of me roared and I knew that I had to kill Keith and keep my word to Mousey. Listen to what I'm saying, cuz, I had to really kill him. What I was gonna do to him was already premeditated. And nobody knew it but me. I got the idea to cut him up from another old friend. When I was in Atlanta in the hole, I ran into a dude from Puerto Rico named Varosso. He told me about how they killed mutha-fuckas in Puerto Rico. He had never walked on the soil here in America. The Puerto Rican prison system put him out of their prisons because he was too strong, too powerful and he did too much killing. One day he told me how he had killed this one dude and made his body disappear.

"He explained how he chopped the dude up as his men held the man and they eventually killed the dude. Varosso says he fully dismembered the dude, then methodically hacked all the skin and meat off his bones. They flushed all the flesh down the toilets piece by piece. He said that they pulverized the bones with hammers. The only thing he said he kept was the dude's skull. That's what I thought about when I heard that Keith was coming here. I wanted to do some shit like that.

"To make a statement to all rats. Like when you snitch, this what you get. I hollered at my AB man in the unit and told him what I needed, and he made it happen. Usually, them AB niggas don't sell weapons to blacks, but he owed me, and I had a little dirt on him that he didn't want getting out, so he made the hatchet for me. The rest was a wrap. Now, I'm just fucked up that I got Ameen and nem caught up in this shit and that Ameen had to take the beef to free us."

"That some real nigga shit, slim did. Taking that beef like that. That nigga like that to do that shit. I respect him to the fullest. You owe slim your life." Goo emphatically replied.

"I already know, cuz, I already know." I thought about the promise I made to Ameen a few days ago in the rec cage. "I can never forget that…never." My mind shifted from the current situation back to the past. I needed to tell my story. To acknowledge my voracious desire to kill. To cleanse my soul. "Cuz, I done did a lot of wild shit, but everything started when I was seven years old. The day I watched my mother die."

"Look at my little man. You so handsome. With all that pretty red hair and them freckles. I swear I don't know where you got 'em from because it damn sure didn't come from your no-good ass daddy. All Fuller ever gave you was a haircut. Old ass nigga. I'm still mad at myself for letting him give you that old ass name. You are too fine to be a Luther. Always make me think about that damn white guy on the old Superman movies. Lex Luther or whatever his name was. That's why I never call you that shit. You been Redds to me ever since you was a baby."

"Can I go outside and play?"

"Go head baby, Mama gotta take her medicine anyway."

"In my eyes, cuz, my mother was the most beautiful and loving creature that God created. But in everybody else eyes she was just a crackhead and a dopefiend. She loved me more than anything except drugs.

"Aye, Peewee, why do all them South West niggas gotta practice on our field up here?" Bean asked.

"Because Greenleaf field is messed up and Randall's is off limits, so the club van be bringing them up here."

"Man, joe, fuck them niggas. Them niggas think shit sweet. Didn't they just jump Larry about a week ago?"

"Yea," Dion replied as he shot two dice on the ground. "Fucked him up, too."

Bean, Worm, Tee, Wayne Wayne, Peewee and Devon sat on the wall next to 501 building. I heard the conversation as I walked up. At 7 years old' I was the youngest out there and Wayne Wayne was the oldest. I followed their eyes as they watched several dudes run football practice drills on the field across from my building.

"Lil Redds, do you think that them niggas should be able

to practice on our field?" Bean asked me.

"Naw, joe," I replied, mimicking the attitude of my friends.

"Aye, Tee, you still got them two guns we found on seventh street, right?"

"You know it." Tee announced, jumped off the wall and sprinted down the block. Minutes later, he was back, holding a brown paper bag in one hand. The bag dropped to the ground after Tee reached in the bag and pulled out two black revolvers.

"Let me see them," I asked excitedly.

"Naw, joe, you too little and too young to be messing with these joints." Tee said and shooed me away as if I was an annoying fly.

"How am I too young and you not? You only two years older than me, Tee. You nine, Bean is 10. Why do yall get to hold them and not me?"

"Maybe next time, Lil Reds." Bean assured. "You can bust one next time. But right now, me and Tee about to get these SW niggas off our field. C'mon, Tee." They walked away from us.

Upset, I walked away from everybody else and went home. On the way I heard what sounded like firecrackers, but I knew it to be gunshots that were coming from the guns out of the brown bag. When I walked in my house it was eerily quiet. I didn't know if the apartment was empty or not, until I walked past the bathroom. The door was ajar, and I could see my mother sitting on the toilet fully clothed. The sleeve of her shirt on the left arm was up and there was a string tied around her arm. A needle was stuck in her arm. My mother's head was thrown back as her eyes rolled around in her head. I thought she was in pain, so I rushed into the bathroom and shook her.

"Ma, wake up! What's wrong with you? Ma! Wake up!"

My mother snapped out of her blue funk, looked at me and said, "Redds, baby, what's wrong? Who Mama gotta beat up?"

Having seen my mother in the mood that she was in and knowing that she was okay, I went into my room to sulk about Bean and nem not letting me hold and fire the guns. About thirty minutes later, I heard the banging on the apartment door. I knew that my mother would get the door, so I just playing video games on the Nintendo 64. Then I heard a man's voice in the living room get louder and louder....

"I'm not playing, Margie! You better gimme my shit!"

"I don't have yall shit. I swear to God, I don't!"

"Chris and Tonya already told me that you stole the stash. Just gimme back my shit, Margie and I'm gone!"

"I don't have it! If Chris and Tonya told yall that, they lying like a muthafucka!"

"Margie, I'm not gonna keep asking you nicely----"

"Nigga, I just told you... 'Whap! Whap! Whap!'

"Gimme my shit, bitch before I kill your stupid ass!"

I got up from game then and looked out my bedroom door. There were two men in the living room. One was wearing a dark colored Sergio Tachinni sweatsuit, he was short and stocky. The other man was taller. He wore jeans and a Madness t-shirt, with white K-Swiss tennis shoes. As I watched, the stocky man smacked my mother repeatedly. I wanted to run out to the living room and defend my mother, but I was afraid to. All I could do was stand there and watch my mother get beat. Then my feet were moving, and my brain was functioning, but I never made it all the way to the living room. I became paralyzed by fear. Ducking into the closet, I shut the door, trying not to be seen. I cracked the door just enough to see. Tears ran down my face, two and three at a time. My mother was now on the floor being beaten and stomped by both men.

"Please...stop," my mother begged.

But nobody listened. I saw the taller man kick my mother's head as it was a ball. Still, I did nothing. Never said a word. All she could do was curl up into the fetal position and beg for her life. All I could was watch. I had never felt so helpless in my life. With one slow powerful kick, I heard my mother's neck snap and saw her body go limp instantly.

"I think she's dead, joe," The tall man said to the stocky one.

"So, what? Fuck her stash stealing ass. She'll learn not to take niggas shit in the next life. Besides that'll send a message to the rest of these junkie muthafuckas that if they steal from us, they get killed."

"I feel you on that, but you do know that Margie is some kin to Marquette, right?"

"I don't give a fuck if she was some kin to Jesus. She stole my shit and got what she deserved. Marquette is gonna have to respect that or check it. If he tryna check it, I'll take his fucking head off and bury it right next to his sister."

Through watery eyes, I watched both men then leave the apartment. Although they were gone, I still stayed in the closet. I knew that my mother was dead and there wasn't a thing that I could do about it. So why come out the closet, I reasoned with myself. Besides that, I was still paralyzed by fear. Fear that caused me to stand by and watch the men kill my mother. Since I hadn't moved to help my mother, I decided right then to never move from that closet again. For the next three days, I didn't move. Didn't eat. Didn't sleep. Didn't go to the bathroom.

I shit my pants and pissed on myself too many times to count. By the fourth day, the apartment smelled horrible and so did I. People knocked on the door repeatedly, but I never answered. Eventually the door to my apartment was kicked in and people spilled in from the hall. I stood in my exact same spot for hours and watched as the police came in, then the EMT, detectives and coroner's office. I watched my mother's body be lifted and taken away.

All the while, nobody bothered to check the hall closet. I was invisible to everybody but myself. I hid from the whole world and couldn't escape the sight of myself, my fear, my cowardice. A few more days turned into nights and still I stood in that closet. My body ached but I ignored the pain. My stomach growled but I ignored that too.

Just when my mind started to meld reality and fiction together, the door to my apartment opened and in walked the person that I thought I would never see again. Kemie. Rakemie Bryant walked around the apartment as if she'd been there a thousand times, but in fact she'd only been inside my apartment twice. As if she was connected to me, she called out my name and then walked directly to the closet. She held her nose against the stench of death and body waste as she opened the closet door.

Kemie's eyes found mine and stared right through to my soul. Tears welled up in her eyes. "Redds, I knew that you were okay. People are saying that whoever killed your mother took you with them. Some people were even saying that you were somewhere dead. But somehow, I knew that you were okay. I just did. Everybody has been looking for you. The school. The cops. The neighborhood. Why---oh my gawd, boy, you stink!"

It was then that I became aware of the smell. My smell.

"C'mon," Kemie said as she grabbed my arm and pulled me from my hiding spot. My legs hurt. I stumbled and fell before rushing back to my feet. "How long have you been in

that closet? What did you see? Why didn't you come out before now?"

I never said a word to Kemie as she continued to bombard me with questions.

"Take your clothes off and get in the bath tub----

I shook my head no. Kemie paid me no mind as she put the stopper in the tub and ran the water. Her disposition was one of a grown woman and not a child like me.

"Boy, I'm not gon look at you. You get undressed and get in the tub. Then you can close the curtain while I sit right here on the toilet and talk to you."

Kemie stepped out of the bathroom and I undressed quickly. Then I got in the tub and closed the curtain. I heard the door open and shut.

"You witnessed it, didn't you?" Kemie asked. "That's why you stayed in the closet. You saw who killed your mother, didn't you?"

For the first time in four days, I spoke. From behind the shower curtain, I could hide while confessing my sins, my shame. "I saw it. I saw what they did to her. I watched her get killed and I didn't do anything to help her." My tears started anew and I told Kemie everything, starting from me being upset because Bean wouldn't let me hold the gun. Once I finished the story, I felt drained. "I could've stopped them. Begged them not to kill her."

"What could you have done, Redds? Fight off two grown men? Get real, boy. If you would've come out of that closet, they would have killed you, too."

"Now I wish that they had killed me, too. How can I live knowing that two men killed my mother and I did nothing?" Before Kemie could answer, I continued, "I should've died with her. I should've said something or did something and I didn't. But I swear to you, now, when I get big, I'ma kill

everybody that had something to do with my mother's death. I put that on my dead mother. Watch. I'ma kill a rack of people."

Sitting in that tub, swearing to avenge my mother, something changed in me. Part of me died with my mother and the hole in my heart became filled with hate and retribution. I thought about something that my homie Damien Lucas once said. "When a man lives in the wolf's den for so long, eventually he learns how to howl. The old me was dead and the new one in his place wanted to howl. It was time to learn how.

Chapter Three

"One, two, one, two, one, two, three. "Damien Lucas called out the combination and I threw the punches. The one punch was my right jab; the two punch was my left jab. And the three punch was my right hook. "Two steps, one, two, weave, come back and slip. One, two, step. One, two, step, weave, come back."

I did exactly as I was instructed by Damien. In my hood Damien Lucas was one of the sharpest fighters around. Nobody could beat him with his hands. Since he was close to my uncle Marquette, he took it upon himself after my mother was killed to teach me how to fight.

"What are you throwing off the jab?"

"The hook."

"When you go downstairs to the body, what do you always do next?"

"Come back up to the head. Body, head. Downstairs, upstairs."

"Skip, catch, weave, comeback. Exactly how I showed you."

"Right."

Damien wiped his head with his shirt bottom and shot an unexpected jab at me. I weaved it easily. He smiled. "Listen young nigga, you're 10 years old now. It's time I showed you something other than how to throw your hands. It's the nineties and niggas is out here killing. It's good to know how to rumble and all that, but it's other shit you gotta learn. C'mon."

I followed Damien to my homie Tee's house. For some reason Tee always held the guns. And I knew that's what Damien wanted to teach me. All about guns. Damien was only 4 years older than me, but his maturity and reputation in the hood made him seem much older. Tee was two years younger than Damien and it showed but to me they were both the big homies. Damien led me into the pantry on the first level of Tee's house. He produced a bag from behind a false wall. In that bag was several guns.

"Guns come in all calibers, sizes and models. There are eight guns in this bag. One snub nose .45 revolver, two automatic .45s, two .38 revolvers, a .380 compact handgun, automatic, one .25 automatic and a .25 revolver. Damien laid all the guns out on the table in the kitchen.

"The two major types of guns are revolvers and automatics. This is a revolver." He picked up one of the .45s and turned it over in his hand. "It's called a revolver because the chamber is a cylinder and it revolves like this. You can spin it. You can look directly into the chamber and see if one of the six are empty. With one of these, they usually only hold six bullets."

Damien picked up each revolver and showed me the revolving cylinders that each held six bullets. "With the revolver, you have to pull the hammer back to start firing. This is how you cock it back. You see that?" I nodded. "You have to cock the hammer back before you attempt to fire a revolver. Once you do that the first time, it will fire one or all 6 bullets. Just depends on how many times you pull the trigger. Now, automatics work a little different. Check this out."

While I watched closely, Damien hit a button on the side of the .45 automatic that ejected the clip. He held the clip in his hand and showed it to me. "The bigger the gun, the less bullets it's likely to hold. This is the .45, a bad motherfucka. It's one of the biggest handguns made. The only ones bigger are .357 automatic and the Desert Eagle .45 and .357. "Aight, check this out. The clip in the .45 holds seven bullets. Now watch this." Damien pulled the top half of the gun and it slid back. "That's how you drop one into the chamber." He ejected the clip back out. "If I put one more bullet in the clip and put it back in the gun, how many bullets would it hold?"

"Eight," I answered quickly. "Seven in the body and one in the head. It's something like boxing."

"That's right youngin', I knew you were a quick study."

Over the next week or so Damien taught me everything there is to know about guns, ammunition, extended clips, beams, mufflers, suppressors, everything. Then when I pretty much had everything learned he rewarded me.

"Here, Redds, this is yours. A gift from me," Damien said and handed me a bundle in a piece of cloth.

I unwrapped the cloth and laid my eyes on the .380 automatic that I had practiced with days before.

"How many bullets does this joint hold?" Damien queried.

"Nine. Ten with a round in the chamber."

"Where the safety at?"

I showed Damien the safety button on the .380.

"Okay, youngin', you know, what you know. But, check this out, you can't tell nobody that I gave this gun to you. Nobody, Bean, Tee, Marquette, Bay One...nobody. You got that?"

"Yeah, I got it, joe."

"Good. Now and go and find somewhere safe to put it. And never show anybody where it is."

****

After my mother was killed, I had an option to move with my father but that would have taken me out the hood and I didn't want to be away from Capers. My aunt Mary also tried to get custody of me but I ran on her and got lost in the streets.

The streets were where I needed to be if I ever wanted to find Chris and Tonya, the crackheads who lied on my mother and got her killed. Several days after the murder, the real story came out. Chris Pike and Tonya Jones stole the dudes Rick and Moody's stash of drugs and blamed it on my mother to save themselves. Rick and Moody. A cocky dude and a tall dude. One wearing a sweatsuit and the other wearing jeans. Two men that I watched kill my mother.

My uncle Marquette was 7 years older than me and I idolized him. To me, he was a hood legend at 14. Most of the time my uncle would take me with him to different chicks houses. His main chick was a bad chick named Tosca that lived in Southwest on a street called Carrollsburg street. Tosca was my first crush and the first girl that I ever seen getting fucked in her ass. I was in love.

One day while with my uncle at her house, I knew what her and my uncle was about to do, so I went outside and ran around to the back of the house. Her bedroom was on the ground floor, so it made my peeping Tom mission successful. Her curtains were always open. I knew because I had watched Quette fuck her on many occasions. Tosca was a pretty chick. She looked like the chick Apollonia from the Purple Rain movie. Her hair was long, her body was bangin', her feet were pretty, and she had a dark, thick patch of pubic hair around her pussy that drove me crazy. I couldn't get enough of Tosca. She had my little young hormones in an uproar. Watching her take that dick in her ass was a dream come true.

"Bend over the bed Tosca and let me get it like that," Quette said.

"No baby, it's gon hurt too bad like that," Tosca said as she pulled her sweatpants down and off. Her red bikini panties came off next. Tosca pulled her shirt over her head, then

*unclasped her red bra. Her breasts spilled all over her chest.
"You gotta do it from the side, Quette. That's the only way I
can take it."*

"A'ight, go 'head and lay on your side then."

"You got the Vaseline, right?!"

"I got it right here," Quette said and showed it to Tosca.

*The way the bed faced, I could see Tosca as she laid on
her side. I could see her facial expressions, her breasts, her
pubic hair and her toes that were polished a bright red color.
I watched my uncle lay directly behind Tosca on his side and
put that dick into her. My dick was bone hard as I watched
Tosca's forehead crease and her teeth bite down on her lip.
She had a wounded, hurt look on her face and it aroused me
to no end.*

*"Quette, do it slow! Owww—owww—Quette—owww—
it hurt! It hurtin' my butt, Quette, you hurting my butt!"*

*"It's already in there, Tosca. Damn, your ass feel so
good."*

*Every time Quette slammed that dick in Tosca's ass, her
toes bent up and her fist gripped the pillow she laid her head
on. That was some sexy shit. I couldn't wait to get some ass.
My uncle was in Tosca's back door for about another five
minutes until he grabbed her and held her. I figured that he
had bust a nut. Something that, at eleven years old, I had yet
to do. I ran back around the house and laughed to myself
about what I'd just seen. Not paying attention to where I was
going, I ran smack into a grown man. He was much bigger
than I was and way more muscular, so when we collided, I
ended up on the ground.*

*"Shorty watch where the fuck you going," the man said
and went to Tosca's front door. Beside the man was a dude
that I recognized immediately. His name was Mark Harris.
A little dark-skinned dude that thought he was hard because*

he hung with the thorough Southwest niggas, Lil Carlton and nem. I immediately mugged on him. He knew what it was with Capers and the West. It was scrap on sight.

"What's up, nigga?" I said to Mark as I got up off the ground.

"You, nigga. What's up with you?" Mark replied, standing his ground.

"Tosca, open the door, bitch," the man said as he pounded on the door. "Open the door."

"Cunta, get the fuck away from my door before I call my father!" Tosca called out.

"Bitch fuck your father. Go 'head and call him. Why you ain't tryna open the door?!"

"Cunta, I don't fuck with you like that no more and you know it."

"You can't never not fuck with a real nigga. How you gon leave me for that coward ass nigga Marquette? Niggas killed his sister and that nigga ain't even do nothing. And he know who did it. You gon leave me for a nigga that can't even protect you?"

"My uncle ain't no coward, nigga!" I said with attitude.

The man looked at me with fire in his eyes. "You lil' bitch nigga, I'll make my son whip your ass."

"You wish. That nigga know what's up with me."

"Nigga, you faking," Mark said.

"You wanna see me Mark?"

"It's whatever."

"Lil Cunta, you better whip that lil red nigga's freckled face ass. If you don't I'ma fuck you up."

Mark rushed me with a slow ass combination that made me laugh. I pivoted and weaved the whole combination. He shot the jab. I caught it and pushed him. Still, I laughed. His fight game was boo-boo. I knew it and he knew it. When he rushed in the next time, I side stepped his jab and caught him with a hook to the body and a straight left to the head. That sat him on his ass.

"Nigga get up and fight," Mark's father shouted.

Before he could get all the way up, I hit him with a combination of punches that had him up against a car, dazed.

"That nigga can't fuck with me," I boasted.

"I respect that shorty. You whipped my son's ass. Now, for that I'ma fuck your uncle up the man told me. He turned to Tosca's door and shouted, "I'ma fuck your car up until you come outside Quette!" The man found a brick and busted out the driver's side window of my uncle's '90 Z. I was mad as shit for two reasons. Because my uncle didn't come outside, and I really liked that car.

"Leave my uncle's car alone, joe!" I hollered at the man.

"Shorty, I will kick your lil young ass. I'm not my son."

"Fuck you and your son, nigga. Ya'll know how us Caper niggas get down."

The man rushed me and grabbed me by my Polo shirt collar.

"Nigga get off me!" I told him.

"Lil smart mouth ass, young nigga...

Pow! Pow! Pow!

I pulled my .380 and started giving my bullets to the man. He tried to run away, but I was on his heels still firing the gun. Pow! Pow! Pow!

"Bitch nigga," I said and then looked around for his son so that I could shoot him, but he was gone.

"My uncle came rushing out of Tosca's house then. "Redds, what the fuck you doing? Put that gun up. Where you get a gun from anyway?" he asked as he pushed me towards the 300 ZX. "Get in the fucking car and don't say shit."

I had to wipe broken glass out of my seat before sitting

down. My uncle sat on his, that's how I knew he was scared. He didn't even feel the broken glass cutting his ass. Back around Capers he had the nerve to be mad at me.

"Why you mad at me?" I asked. "All I did was defend you."

"Defend me? Nigga, you eleven years old, how you gon defend me?"

"The way I did. You had that big black nigga talking greasy to you, unc, I had to do something. 'Specially when he said what he said about my mother. Then he put his hands on me. Why you ain't do nothing to him?"

"Cause I wasn't out there," Quette argued.

"You wasn't tryna be out there." I thought as I sulked on the sidewalk. "He got what he was looking for if you ask me."

"Well, nobody asked you." my uncle pouted and walked away.

I walked down the street and around the corner until I reached Kemie's house. She was outside on the porch with her cousin Reesie and her friend Marnie.

"Kemie, let me talk to you," I said from the gate.

"Hi Redds!" Marnie and Reesie both called out.

"What's up, Reesie. What's up Marnie," I responded back.

Kemie came off the porch and out the fence. I grabbed her and hugged her. "What's up, young? You missed me?" I asked her.

"You know I always miss you, boy. I'm supposed to miss my boyfriend."

"Boyfriend? I though you go with Kevin, Larry's brother?"

"Boy, stop playing. I don't like his big head butt."

"That's what I heard."

"Well, you heard wrong. Why you haven't been to

school?"

"Fuck school. Vanness can't teach me how to live out here on these mean streets. Unless they can tell me how to make explosives."

"Explosives? Redds, you be lunching like shit."

"But you love me though, right?"

"Uh huh, I do. I don't even know why."

I took Kemie's hand and put it on my dick. "I know why."

She quickly snatched her hand back. "Don't be doing that here. Putting my hand on your lil thing."

"Ain't nothing little about my thing. You saw it before."

"And that was one time too many."

Thinking about Tosca getting hit in the ass made me aggressive. "When you gon stop fakin' and give me some coochie? I been waiting for a long time already."

"And you gon keep waiting. I'm not giving you none of my stuff until I turn sixteen. The day I turn sixteen it's all yours."

"You promise?"

"I promise."

"Okay. And what about that lil phat butt?"

"What?"

"That butt? I'm tryna get some of that butt then, too. You got me?"

"Hell no!" Kemie exploded. "That's some nasty stuff boy. I ain't never letting nobody put their thing in my butt. That ain't what the butt is for. It's an exit, not an entrance."

"Yeah, whatever...."

"Redds! Redds!" Esha came around the corner calling my name. Dawn on her heels.

"What's up, Esha?" I asked her.

"Who the hell did you shoot, boy?" Esha asked out of breath. "Kemie, Redds shot somebody down Southwest."

"Redds, what is Esha talking about? You shot somebody!"

I told everybody present the story about what happened earlier.

"Them boys from down there is riding around looking for you," Dawn said.

"It's two cars full of niggas that keep riding around here. They asked Pee Wee where Marquette was at and then they asked about you," Esha piped in. "They gon get your lil ass, Redds."

"Ain't nobody gon do nothing to me," I replied and pulled out my gun. "Boy, my mother and my aunt is in the house. If they look out here and see you waving that gun around, I'ma get in trouble and you aint gon never be allowed to come over here again. What the hell are you doing with a gun anyway?"

Just about to say some slick shit to Kemie, I remembered that I was outta bullets. The thought of getting shot and couldn't shoot back didn't appeal to me, so I took off running down the street. It didn't take me long to get to Tee's house and load my gun with ammo. By the time I got back around the way, a large crowd had gathered on I street. When I approached, all eyes were on me.

"There go shorty right there," Cunta said to his men.

I heard somebody with him say, "That lil' ass boy shot you?"

"Yeah, I shot his bitch ass," I announced aggressively. My gun gave me the heart of a giant. I tried to step out into the street but was held back by Bean.

"Chill out, Redds."

"Shorty, you gon make me…I'm tryna see Marquette for what his nephew did to me. He gotta see me," Cunta said.

Damien, Dion, Moosy, E-man, Bill, Crump, big Gerald, Creeko and a lot of other older duds from the hood were outside.

"Quette ain't out here, slim. So, how he gon see you?"
Creeko said.

"Well, somebody gon see me. Shorty that shot me—

"Ain't gon happen, young." Damien Lucas stepped up
and said. "Shorty is a youngin', he like eleven or twelve. And
he's like a brother to me. Quette ain't here but I am. Ain't
nobody gon touch lil Redds out here. Yall niggas coming up
here looking for niggas, talking 'bout you tryna see niggas
and shit, like we sweet or something. I understand though,
because a lotta yall SW niggas is dumb as shit. Yall should
know better. But since yall don't, I'm about to show yall.
Quette ain't out here, but I am and I'm tryna see anyone or
all of y'all one on one. What's up?"

"Nigga, fuck, is you? Talking that tough shit. Let's do it,"
Cunta said and bent down to tie his shoes.

Everybody circled the two fighters and gave them room
to go toe to toe. I knew that Damien was a beast with his
hands and that nobody could beat him in a fight. But the SW
niggas, mainly Cunta, must didn't know that. I watched Da-
mien feel the dude out, all the while, itching to pull out my
gun and start blasting.

Bean saw my movements and read my mind exactly. Then
he put his arm across my chest and said, "Chill out, joe. Eve-
rybody know by now that you'll bust that hammer. But you're
not a killer yet. And they are---" Bean gestured towards the
crowd that was with Cunta. "That's Vito Hill, Sam Carson,
Raymond Washington, Pimp, Poo Poo and Lil Draper. Their
guns are a little bigger than yours lil homie."

"But is their heart like mine?" When Bean didn't reply,
I said, "Fuck them niggas. all of 'em."

The next thing I knew, Cunta was on the ground knocked
out cold from a Damien Lucas three-piece that caught him

flesh.

"Pick y'all man up and get him outta here. Or does one of y'all wanna go next?" Damien gloated.

"Another time, joe. Another time," Vito Hill said. Then they gathered their fallen comrade and left.

Chapter Four

"Happy Birthday, Redds!" Bay One called out as I walked through her front door.

"Thanks, Bay. What you got for me?" I joked. "Them new Dennis Rodman tennis shoes?"

Bay One pulled a shoe box out from under her seat. The box had a Nike logo on it. "Somebody ratted me out, didn't they?"

"Naw," I said and laughed.

"Well, how did you know that I was getting you Rodman's for your birthday? Never mind. I already know that it was Esha's dry snitching ass. Try 'em on and see if you like 'em."

"I don't have to try 'em on, they are a seven and a half. That's my size and I already know that I like 'em. Thanks, Bay. I appreciate you. No bullshit." I walked over to Bay One and hugged her.

"Don't mention it, baby boy, you family. But you twelve not twenty, so you better watch your mouth around me. In here cussin' and shit like you grown."

"My bad, Bay. But thanks again for the shoes, they gon look tight with the outfit that Damien bought me."

Bay One shook her head and laughed. "Everybody is always buying you shit."

"Because I'm a good young nigga. That's why."

"Nigga, ain't nothing good about your lil bad ass. Shooting people and shit. Damn, I wish your mother could be here to see how fine your lil red ass done grew up to be. I heard you got all the lil young bitches."

"Jive like. They be on me, but I ain't trippin' off all that right now. But speaking of my mother, do you know a broad

named Tonya Jones, Bay?"

"Yeah, I know her crack smoking ass. Why? What's up with her?"

"Nothing much, I just heard through the grapevine over the years that she was the one who told them dudes that my mother stole their stash. I heard that her some nigga named Chris Pike lied on my mother to get the heat off the fact that they stole them dude's shi---stuff."

"I think I did hear some shit like that years ago, but I never really paid it no mind. Tonya still around. She works at the Mirage nightclub as a bartender. And Chris is a security guard now at the Safeway in Waterside Mall."

"Is that right? So close, yet so far away."

"What the hell are you talking about, boy?"

"Nothing, Bay, I'm just talkin'. Where Esha at?"

"Upstairs." Bay said, got up off the couch and headed for the door. "I'll see y'all later."

"A'ight, Bay. Later."

I ran up the stairs and walked in Esha's room without knocking. She was sitting on the bed polishing her toenails light purple. "What's up. Esh?"

"Damn, boy, don't be busting all up in here like that. What if I would have been naked or something?"

"That would mean that you was looking out for a young nigga on his birthday."

"Yeah, boy, whatever. What you want?"

"Nothing. I just came to holla at you and tell you that I think your mother wanna give me some pussy." Esha jumped up, spilling polish on her bed. She grabbed a pillow and slung it at me. "Why you do that?"

"I should do more than that. Redds, don't be playing with my motherfuckin' mother like that."

"Anybody ever told you that you curse too much to be 15

years old?"

"Fuck you. How 'bout that. Anybody ever told you fuck you before and meant it?"

"Fuck you, too, then. You know I was just playing. Everybody in the world know that Bayona Lake ain't giving no man that pussy. We know how Bay get down."

"That's y'all problem around here. Everybody know too damn much, or think they know a lot and in all actuality y'all don't know shit. Need to mind y'all business. You can leave now. You saw me. You said what's up. Now get out. Making me spill this polish on my sheets."

"My bad. I can buy you some sheets. I ain't broke."

"Whatever, Redds. How old did you turn today?"

"Thirteen."

"Stop lying. You turned twelve."

"If you already knew that, why ask me?"

"Redda, get your lil' red ass outta my room. Before I---"

"Before you what, Esh? And ain't nothing little about me. They should call me big Redds."

"Yeah, right. Get your lil' ass on somewhere. Ain't nothing big about you but your ego and your mouth and I'm tired of hearing it.

I felt like Esha was trying to diss me and I wasn't feeling that. I had to prove my manhood in a different way. I went to Esha's door and acted like I was leaving, but at the door, I shut it and locked it. The look on Esha's face was one of confusion as I pulled my sweatpants down and pulled my dick out my underwear. I stroked a few times and shook it." Like, I said, ain't shit little about me."

The nail polish slipped from Esha's hand again but didn't spill. Her eyes were as big as silver dollars. "Got damn, boy, where you get all that dick from? Mr. Fuller? Because it damn sure wasn't your mother's side. Quette dick ain't nowhere near that big."

A sly smile crossed my face. "How do you know how big my uncle's dick is? You gave him the coochie?"

"Wouldn't you like to know? Remember what I said earlier about people minding their business? Well, do that. And besides everybody in Capers projects know that Marquette Henderson like young bitches."

"Tosca ain't young. She gotta be at least twenty."

"Well, there's always an exception to the rule. Like you. You're an except---well, not just you. Worm dick is big as shit, too, for him to be so young. So, both of yall are exceptions to the rule. Young and packing like shit. And speaking of packing, I didn't get you no gift for your birthday yet, so what do you want?"

There I was standing in Esha's room with my dick in my hand and she was asking me what I want. Dressed in nothing but a long shirt. Occasionally, I could see a hint of her underwear color. Purple. I wondered to myself whether, or not her question was a trick one. "You gon give me whatever I ask for?"

"I might," Esha said brushing at the spilled polish on her sheets. "Depends on what you ask for."

"I know you gon laugh me out or kirk on me, but fuck it, I'ma shoot my shot. Ever since my mother was killed, your mother been like a godmother to me and we been on some brother and sister shit. But fuck all that, Esh. I'm tryna get some pussy. Kemie keep talkin' that 'we too young for sex' shit and I ain't with fucking no crackheads and dopefiends. I'm out in the streets doing everything under the sun but fucking and I'm tired of it. I can't be a gangsta and a virgin. That shit ain't proper."

Esha looked up at me, still stroking my dick. "Well, I guess you right about the gangsta and virgin part. I think I can help you out. But boy, I swear to God, if you tell anybody what we about to do, I will deny it and start all kinds of rumors about you. Do you hear me?"

"How can I not hear you and you talk loud as shit. I'm not gonna tell anybody anything. You can believe that. Loose lips sink ships. Damien taught me that."

"Damien taught you that, huh?" Esha said as she pulled the shirt over her head, exposing her breasts and purple panties. "Well, Esha's about to teach you something, too."

I watched as Esha slipped her legs out of the panties one at a time. She was phat as shit and I couldn't believe what was happening. Esha rubbed her hands all over her body and stopped at her center. Her pubic hair was a little beady, but other than that she was bad.

My eyes almost popped out of my head. I couldn't believe what had just happened. Never in my life did I think Esha would give me some pussy. Her skin was dark and flawless. Her breasts weren't that big, but they were pretty. The best thing about Esha to me was her mouth. Her lips were luscious, and she had the prettiest smile in the world.

"Take your clothes off" Esha told me. "All of 'em."

"You ain't gon lock the door?" I asked.

Esha walked past me and locked her bedroom door. "What's taking you so long? Let me find out your lil tough ass scared."

"I asked you for some pussy, so how I'ma be scared?"

Esha stood beside the bed and watched as I completely disrobed. I was ready to become a man in the literal, sexual sense.

"Lay on the bed and let me do everything. I'ma teach you how to not only sex a woman----

"You ain't no woman. You young like me."

"Boy, shut up and lay down. I am a woman and I'm not

young like you. I'll be fifteen in two months. That ain't young. But anyway, I'ma teach you how to make a woman cum. You ever seen a man eat some pussy?"

"Naw. Oh, yeah, yeah, I saw Marquette eating Tosca one time."

"They did that in front of you?"

I couldn't tell Esha about my peeping Tom ways, so I lied. "Yeah, so what?"

Esha stood up in the bed and put a leg on each side of my body. Then she walked up towards my face. I laid my head on the pillow and looked straight up at her standing above me. The beady hairs on her pussy gave way to a phat, pink pussy. I'd never seen one so close-up before. I stared at its size and shape in disbelief. I was in even more disbelief when she squatted over my face and put the pussy on my lips. To my surprise if smelled good, like soap.

"Stick your tongue out Redds. When I move my pussy over your lips, you gotta stick your tongue out and let me ride your tongue."

I didn't have a clue as to what Esha was talking about, but I did as she instructed. My tongue came in contact with her pussy and Esha moved all over my face like a snake. Whatever I was doing, I was doing it good because Esha started moaning and making a rack of noise. Then I felt my face get extra wet.

"Damn Redds, you just made me cum, boy. Damn!"

"In my mouth? On my face? Fuck you do that for?" I argued.

"Boy, just chill out. I'm about to do you so you can cum in my mouth" Esha said while getting off my face.

"She crawled down to the end of the bed and came up between my legs. My dick stood straight up." "Ain't nobody never sucked this dick before, huh?"

Naw. I told you I ain't with tricking shit."

"Good. Lay back and watch me work this joint. I'm a beast."

True to her word, Esha sucked my lil' young dick like a professional prostitute. I laid back on that bed, with my hands behind my head, and watched Esha work. At some point I couldn't watch anymore because it felt too good. I closed my eyes and shook my feet. My toes were curling, and it made me get scared. I had never in my life felt anything like what Esha was doing. My body did shit on its own like move when I didn't tell it to move.

"I felt a feeling deep in my body and it made me feel like I needed to pee. It built up and built up and I couldn't stop it Then on its own, I let the pee out while moaning like hell. Esha rose up off my dick and kept stroking it. I looked down my body and saw the liquid that came out and it wasn't piss. It was cum. I had finally busted a nut. I was siced. "What the fuck, Esh? I felt like I peed on myself."

"Did it feel good?" Esha asked me.

"Hell yeah, that shit was like that."

"I told you I'ma beast."

"Who taught you that shit?" I asked curiously.

"I can't tell you that."

"You do it a lot?"

"Practice makes perfect. That's what they say."

"Can you practice on me a couple more times?"

"I'll think about it," Esha said, still rubbing and licking my soft dick. "But right now, you need to get this lil' guy back together so that I can put this pussy on you."

Just thinking about fucking Esha made my dick grow in her hand. I was ready for round two. Esha was too, because at the sight of my erection, she rose up again and stood over my mid-section. Then she squatted down until she was *almost sitting. Esha took my dick and rubbed the head around her pussy for a minute and then she sat down on it slowly.*

"Awww—shit---boy! Your lil'ass----damn---." Esha lowered herself completely onto my dick.

"I watched it disappear inside her tight pussy and then closed my eyes. I felt Esha's hands on my chest. Her nails dug into my flesh as she bounced up and down slowly. The feeling was indescribable to me. Her pussy was soaking wet and it made noises as she rode me.

"Damn Redds! Your lil'---young ass---dick all big and shit----awww shit---damn----boy---awwww shit!" Esha moaned in ecstasy. "Oooh---ooh---you lil ass---damn---dick---good as---shit. Fuck---damn---shit---ooooh---I'm 'bout to---cum---cum---all—on it. Redds---oooh shit---boy!"

I opened my eyes to watch Esha. Just seeing her on top of me, riding me, her facial expressions one of pain and hurt, that made me wanna fuck her for a long time. I didn't want to cum again and the experience be over with. I needed it to last. Plus, I wanted to try something that I saw my uncle do. "Hold on, Esha, stop!"

Esha's eyes opened and she asked, "Why, what's wrong?"

"Ain't shit wrong. I just want to change positions. Let me get up." Esha rose up off my dick. I stood up and got off the bed. "Get on your hands and knees. I wanna do it to you like that."

Esha smile. "You want this pussy from the back? Okay." She got up, walked to the back of the bed, then climbed up on it and got on all fours.

I did as I saw my uncle do and step up behind her and put my dick back in her. Esha looked over her shoulder at me as I went in deep. The face she made was priceless. I grabbed her waist and pounded into her until a few moments later I busted a nut, and I never pulled my dick out. "You bout to be my baby mother, Esha."

Esha laid down flat on her stomach and exhaled. "Whew! That was like that. Your lil ass ain't busting no baby makers, boy. Not yet anyway. I know one thing though, your lil young ass gon have all the bitches. Lil big dick ass.

My dick was wet and it smelled---I smelled like pussy. But I didn't care and I didn't want to wash the smell off of me. I wanted to wear the smell like a badge of honor. I had finally got some pussy and I couldn't wait to tell my boys.

Anthony Fields

Chapter Five

"Lil Redds," Damien called out. "C'mere."

*Damien leaned on the back of his 4 door Acura Legend.
Its system blasted 'California Love'. I walked across the
street to the car. "What's up, Dee?"*

*"Ain't shit, youngin'. I'm just wondering why you walk-
ing around here with your face all balled up. What's up with
you?"*

*"I'm cool, joe. Just fucked up in the head because I let
Bean take all my money shooting dice. That's all."*

"Do you even know how to shoot dice?" Damien asked.

"Of course, I do," I replied.

*"We'll see about that. Here," Damien pulled out a wad
of money and counted out ten hundred-dollar bills and
passed them to me. "Put this in your pocket."*

*I snatched the bills eagerly out of Damien's hand. The
only thing on my mind was getting my money back from Bean.
But before I could run off Damien stopped me.*

*"Not so fast, youngin. Get in the car. There's a few things
you gotta learn and after today, if I ever catch you broke
again, I'ma stop fuckin' with you."*

*Damien was quiet on the ride to Stanton Hill apartments
on the other side of Southeast. He never said a word. In the
complex, I followed him to an apartment in one the buildings
on the second floor. Damien knocked on the door. Seconds
later a beautiful, jet black woman with long braids and
braces on her pearl white teeth opened the door. We walked
past her to the kitchen. There Damien pulled out a pair of
dice.*

*"Listen, youngin', it's three things in this world that's
gon keep some money in your pocket. So, after today, if
you're ever broke again, I ain't fuckin with you no more. You*

feel me? I never want to feel like I'm wasting my time when I teach you shit. Like I was saying, there's three things that you can have that will make money. Dice, drugs and your gun. I say your gun because if the dice and the drugs ain't working for you, you can always just take money. Let other niggas make it and you take it. But, see youngin, you gotta be multi-faceted. That word might be too big for you right now, but one day you'll understand it completely. For now, it just means that you gotta be able to do a few different things well and not just one. You got regular stick up niggas and that's all they do, but a lot of time you'll find them niggas broke as shit. Why? Because they aint's got a secondary hustle. They have one. You gon have all three. Like me." For the next hour or so, Damien taught me everything he could about the dice. He taught me how to swirl them, twirl them, set them, lick them, walk them, pod roll them, shoot them up against a wall. He taught me everything.

"And you gotta be able to recognize a shark, youngin. That's a nigga who gambles to eat. If he don't win, he don't eat. You gotta recognize loaded dice and trick dice. You gotta watch for the 'switch.' Niggas switch good dice for bad ones in a heartbeat. In most cases the hands are quicker than the eyes." Next came my schooling on drugs.

"Weed is a good hustle, youngin, but you gotta be the connect to get paid. Take them niggas down the West. They got Delaware Avenue jumping off a dub bags of weed. Why? Because their dubs are bigger than everybody else's. Why? Because them niggas are getting weed from Arizona. They driving the shit in. They going to Arizona paying like a hundred or less a pound. Back here in DC they selling that same pound for a grand. The young niggas outside on the curb is making about eighth-hundred dollars off the pound after recouping their grand. Feel me? If you gon sell weed, never be* *the nigga outside all day going hand to hand. The jump outs gon bag you on a regular. The nigga who well the pounds is the nigga you never see. He got all the cake."*

Damien showed me powdered coke and how to cook it both ways. With water and without. He was like a real chemist or a mad scientist to me. I was completely in awe.

"Some rules apply for the coke, youngin'. Sell weight or nothing at all. Hand to hand is a no go. Save your money, buy powder, cook it and sell weight to your men. Sell 'em eight-balls and quarters, fourteen grams or the whole twenty-eight. Or you can give 'em a wholesale." I was a great student, soaking up everything Damien said like a sponge.

"I just gave you a thousand dollars outside before we came here. Do you wanna spend seven hundred on some coke already cooked up or do you wanna spend nine-hundred on some powder coke?"

"I'll take the powdered coke because I can cook it myself, with little to no water and stretch it out. Instead of giving you seven-hundred for twenty-eight grams, I'll pay the extra two-hundred for the twenty-eight that I can turn into forty grams."

All Damien could do was smile. He gave me an ounce of powder coke and I gave him nine of the hundred-dollar bills that he'd given me.

"Now, youngin', lastly---but this is by far your most important lesson. But before I teach it to you, let's go in the back right quick." He led me to a back room that wasn't furnished. All it contained was a safe and a metal lockbox next to it. Damien opened the lockbox. It was full of guns and ammo. "I can't keep this shit at Tee's house no more." Damien told me. "The nigga keep taking my shit." He reached into the box and pulled out a handgun. "It's time to upgrade you, youngin'. "Here, take this." He handed me the gun.

I turned it over in my hands as if I could feel its power surging through me. "That's a T nine-millimeter. Pop the clip out and you'll see that it holds sixteen bullets. So, now you've got a seventeen shot nina. I'ma give you a box of bullets for it, too. Now follow me."

I followed Damien outside and around the apartment building. In the back of the building was two kennels. In one kennel, there was a red nose, cocaine white pit bull and small baby pits. In the other cage was a lone pit bull, also a red nose, but it was beige with white spots.

"This is my bitch," Damien said pointing at the white pit bull. "She go hard as shit. Ain't never lost a fight. But him," *Damien pointed at the other pit bull. "He's more bitch than her. I fought him yesterday and lost a rack of money fucking with him. This nigga got into some serious shit with another pit from up the street and when we broke the two pits up, I held him. When the dude that was calling the dog fight yelled, "Break!" I let this nigga go and he didn't move. The bitch nigga wouldn't come out the corner. I lost by default. I raised this pit, youngin' and don't get it twisted, we made a rack of money together. And I love this nigga like a brother. But the pit has given up on himself. He's a bitch. Now, check this out. All that wild ass shooting up shit you been doing, that stops today.*

"All you doing is wasting bullets. I hate wasting bullets and time. If somebody makes you mad enough to shoot at him, then be mad enough to kill him. It's just that simple. If you pull the gun use it. Somebody fuck up, get rid of 'em. If they cross you, kill 'em. They hurt you, kill 'em. Don't ever shoot to maim. Shoot to kill. Walk your man down, chase him down, or surprise him, just make sure you don't leave a wounded enemy around to come back for you.

"Do whatever it takes to end all beefs. There's no such

thing as a halfway beef. If you have to wait, be patient and get your man, whoever he may be. Don't have no picks. None. If I crossed you, you shouldn't hesitate to kill me. That's just the way it goes. There may come a time when you have to kill those you love."

Damien opened the door to the kennel and called out to the red nose, cocaine white pitbull. "Here, girl," The pitbull came out and lowered her head to rub it on Damien's leg. Without a moment hesitation, Damien pull a gun from his waist and shot the white pit in the head.

I jumped from the sound of the gun and the suddenness of what Damien had done.

Damien walked over to the second kennel and let the beige pit out. "Kill him, Redds."

With no remorse, I pulled the Taurus and shot the beige pit in the head.

"That's right, youngin'. I knew you had it in you. The way you did the dog is the way you kill anybody that gets in your way. Man, woman or child." Damien reached in the kennel and grabbed one of the pitbull puppies and handed it to me. "Here, take one. Take care of her." Then he killed all the baby pits, one by one.

"Dee, I understand why you told me to kill the beige pit, but why did you kill the white pit and all the puppies?"

We left the kennel and the dead dogs and walked back to the parking lot. At the car, Damien said, "The white bitch loved that coward ass beige pit. I didn't want you to kill him while she watched, so I killed her first. Remember what I told you. Sometimes we kill the ones we love. I killed the puppies because of their father. He was a bitch and they had his genes. They would have grown up to be just like him."

"Well, why did you give this one to me? If it's gonna grow up to be like the father?"

"Don't let it grow up to be like the father. Make him grow up to be like you."

"He gon be a killer then."

"We'll see, youngin'. We'll see."

Chapter Six

"When I was young, me and my mama had beef/ seventeen years old kicked out in the street/ and back at the time I never thought I'd see her face/ ain't no woman alive that can take my mama place..."

"Excuse me, ma'am? Can you spare a little change?"

"Here you go, baby." The woman said and dropped 3 quarters into my open palm.

I looked over my shoulder to make sure that I was in plain view of the entrance to Safeway. At some point, I knew that the security guard was gonna come out and run me away and that's what I wanted. Sure enough, 15 minutes later, he did just that.

"You can't be out here panhandling, shorty. The people who own this joint don't want yall young niggas on the property, begging and shit. You gotta roll out."

Quickly, I read the badge on the guard's shirt. Pike. C. Pike. "Aight, you got that. But can you please help me get my bike?"

"Get your bike? Get your bike from where?"

"It's on the side of the store, somebody hit the small tree back there and it fell on my bike. I can't lift the tree by myself, I need a little help. Please help me, officer so I can go home."

"A'ight, shorty, c'mon. Where your bike at?"

"On the side of the store. I always leave it right there while I'm hustling. But the lil' tree done fell on it." I lead the security guard around to the side of the building. It was getting dark outside and I welcomed the cover of darkness.

"Where your bike at?" The security guard asked.

"Right over there in the cut," I replied and whipped out the Taurus. I was walking directly beside the security guard to his right, so he never saw my concealed weapon. "Hey,

officer? Do you remember a lady named Margaret Henderson? Everybody called her Margie?"

The security guard's neck moved as if it was on a swivel. His eyes grew large and followed my arm to the end of my wrist and the gun. I stopped in my tracks and pointed the gun at Chris Pike. He looked to be in good shape and no longer a crackhead.

"Yea...I know...knew Margie. What's going on here, shorty? Why you got a gun out?"

"Because you and a broad named Tonya lied on my mother about some drugs and got her killed."

"That wasn't me. That was Tonya's shit. I didn't tell Rick and nem shit. Tonya took their shit and told them it was Margie."

I looked at dude and saw the fear in his eyes. My heart rate sped up. The Taurus felt heavy in my hand. I thought about everything Damien had said to me a week ago. And I thought about the dog. The security guard was the dog. "It doesn't matter who told the lie. It was told, you was with it and my mother died because of it."

I raised the gun and fired until it was empty. The firing pen hitting an empty chamber snapped me out of my daze. I stood over Chris Pike and saw the holes in his head and the trickles of blood exiting them. I had killed my first man and I had to admit that I loved it. Craved it.

****

"What time do that joint let out?"

"I heard it let out at like three," Bean said and laid back on the front porch of the green house directly across from the Mirage nightclub.

"The music loud as shit. I wonder what band that is

playing."

"You stupid as shit, young. You can't hear that that's Essence in there?"

"Fuck Essence. It's Junkyard band all day with me. What time is it?"

"It's two-fifty-five am."

"The broad Tonya probably won't be out until after all the people cleared the spot. Bay One said she's a bartender, so she probably gotta clean the bar and a rack of other shit. You say you remember what she looks like, right?"

"Didn't I tell your geekin' ass three times already, I know what she looks like. I'm surprised that you don't remember her. All that coke she smoked in your hallway. Tonya Jones is some kin to Noel and nem."

"I can't remember her, joe. But either way, it don't even matter. Her ass is outta here as soon as she exits that building."

"So, you dead serious about killing her, huh?' Bean asked.

"Watch my work."

Bean walked up to the chubby lady as she walked down the street. I watched as he talked to her for a few minutes. I came off the porch and walked towards them. The woman that he stopped and conversated with was my target. Without saying a word, I walked up behind the chubby woman and blew her brains out. I stayed to watch her body fall, but that's it. It was time to go.

"Young, your lil ass vicious." Bean complimented.

Sirens sounded in the night as cars raced to the scene not far from the Mirage nightclub. I pulled off the hood that I wore and replaced it with a long sleeve Polo shirt. The gun I tucked in my waist. "I told you I was gon crush her ass. No talk, all action."

"I can't let you outdo me, joe. I'm killing me a mutha-fucka soon. I don't know who it's gonna be yet, but I'm doing it. Then you can watch my work."

Chapter Seven

"You hacking me like shit." Tubby complained.

Joe London knew that Tubby was gonna cry the whole basketball game. It never failed. Tubby did it every time. "Stop all that muthafucking crying, young. If you ain't tryna get touched, don't come in the paint. Take the ball out."

"Fuck you nigga----" Bok. Bok. Bok. Bok.

Boom! Boom! Boom! Boom!

"What the fuck?" That was what I said to myself right before my feet got the signal from my brain to run. I ran. Ended up behind a parked van. When the gunshots rang out everybody scattered and ran for cover. It was the natural re-action for people who grew up in the hood. When the shots stopped, everybody came from their hiding spot. It was then that I remembered the gun on my waist. I could have returned fire and didn't. "Never again."

An ear piercing scream shattered the afternoon sky. A small crowd gathered around somebody laying on the ground. Nobody made any attempts to call an ambulance and that wasn't a good sign. My mind searched the crowd for all my men and they were all accounted for. As I reached the crowd and peered through to see who was on the ground, a woman fainted. It was my homie E-Man's mother Naomi. The big homie from my building had been killed instantly. Bullets from a large caliber weapon had blown half of his face completely off.

****

"Them SW niggas did that shit." Somebody was saying as soon as me and Bean walked into Bay One's house.

"How do you know that?" Red Moosey asked.

"I was in my window when they drove up in the black caravan. They got out the van through the side door with

guns out, walked up to the basketball court and started shooting." Lisa Bell explained. "It was fat Swison, Dirty Paul and Hard Rock."

"Lisa, are you 100 percent sure it was them?" Creeko queried.

"I went to Jefferson Jr. High with all 3 of them. I can spot them out of a crowd from anywhere. It was them. After they finished shooting, they ran back to the black van and it pulled off."

"Was E-Man beefing with them niggas?" Fat Rat asked Creeko.

"Not that I know of. E-Man probably wasn't even the target. I think they still mad about what Damien did to Cunta and how he called them out and ain't nobody do nothin'."

I had heard enough. E-Man was the big homie who always gave me dollars and shit when I was coming up. His sister Weasel used to babysit me when my mother was gonna be in the streets for a long time. His mother was my mother's best friend. There's was no way that I could let what happened to E-Man slide. One thing that I had learned from being in the hood was that my older homies were slow to act and they were a little scared at times if they knew that things would get messy and bloody. Countless times, I had watched them side step certain beefs because the opponents were reputable and strong. But me, I didn't give a fuck. Having witnessed my mother's murder and doing nothing to help her, my conscience, my humanity, my compassion, my soul...they were all gone. A hollow void left to take their place. I tapped Bean and motioned for him to follow me out of the house. Outside, I told Bean, "We gotta get back about E-Man, joe. You know how them niggas in there is. When it's some small shit, they'll step to it, but when it's time to kill niggas, they be bullshittin'. I ain't down for the bullshittin'. E-Man looked out for me and he didn't deserve that shit. You told me the other day that you were ready to kill, right? You said that I'ma have to watch your work, right?"

"Yea, that's what I said. And I meant it. What's up?"

"You already know. The same thing I did to Tonya Jones."

"Let's do it. It's gonna be just me and you?"

"Naw. We gotta take a few more people. Somebody to drive and somebody else to shoot. Who you think will bust that gun and don't fold up?"

Me and Bean looked at each other and smiled. Then in unison, we said, "TJ."

James Creek Dwellings was one of the three most dangerous projects in Southwest DC. But I could care less. Devon parked the stolen Toyota Camry on Half Street across from Syphax Elementary. It was late in the evening, but we knew that there would be people outside in the projects. Good for us, bad for them. Guns cocked, locked and loaded, I surveyed the scene and saw several dudes standing in an alley off of N street.

"TJ, you ready, young?" Bean asked.

"I'm ready, joe." TJ replied. "Who am I suppose to shoot?"

"Everybody." I announced. "Lisa said that the dudes who shot E-Man were Dirty Paul, Swison and Hard Rock. Since we don't know who them niggas is, we shoot everybody and hope we kill one of them. Let's go."

Bean stopped me by pulling my arm. "We can't just walk in the alley with guns out, they'll run. Let's go down by Friendly's and come through the cut that leads to where they are. We'll surprise them."

I nodded my head and glanced at TJ. He shrugged at me. "Let's go."

Five minutes later, we had the element of surprise on

about seven dudes and two females.

"Where did them bitches come from?" Bean asked.

"Fuck them, joe. Anybody can get it. Hit they ass, too."

We walked out into the open like we belonged in that alley. Since we were youngins nobody really paid us any mind. Their mistake. I raised my gun and fired at everybody standing in that alley. One dude dropped to the ground holding his stomach while others fled. I ran down on the fallen dude and looked in his face. His eyes pleaded for mercy. I had none to give. I fired a shot into his forehead. I glanced around and saw TJ and bean standing over dudes as well firing shots. One of the females lay on the ground screaming. I quickly crossed over to her and shot her several times. All I could think about was killing. Anybody and everybody. I needed to kill. To cleanse myself of the cowardice that lived inside me. The cowardice that made me stay in a closet pissy and shitty for days while my mother's corpse lay not even three feet away. We ran back to the Camry and Devon pulled off with the tires screeching.

Back around the way, we discussed the murders.

"Did yall see me crush that nigga?" TJ boasted. "I fucked his ass up. All head and face shit."

"Yea, I saw you, youngin'. You did good." Bean said. "How does it feel?"

"It feels good."

"Yea, for me, too. It felt good to me."

I listened to Bean and TJ, but really paid them no mind. I couldn't stop thinking about the holes that the bullets made in that girl's head as I killed her.

Early the next morning, at least ten police cars came from every direction and blocked off every corner and cut on 7th street. Uniformed and plainclothed officers swarmed us. They grabbed me, Bean, TJ and Worm.

"Fuck I do?" Worm exploded. "Yall grabbing me and I ain't even do nothing. Bean, tell these cops that I wasn't with yall.'

I heard Bean hiss, "Hot ass nigga."

All I could do as I was cuffed was shake my head. How had we been identified that fast? Who were the witnesses?

"Are you sure this is them, Sarge?" one cop asked the other that had me by the arm. "These are kids. Ain't no way they did that shit in the alley."

The Sargent looked at some papers on a clip board. "They fit the description. Witnesses say the shooters were teens. They found the stolen getaway vehicle around the corner. I'd bet you a dime to a donut that at least one of these guys prints are in it. Besides, it's our job to arrest and the courts job to figure out guilt or innocence."

By nightfall, the local media had made a big deal about the four juveniles allegedly responsible for the four brutal murders of three men and one teenage girl. Our names and faces couldn't be used on the news because of our ages, but the commotion stirred up emotions on the streets. Blood quickly spilled on both sides of the beef. All the while I was held in a small cell at the Receiving Home for Children, a juvenile detention center in Northeast. Since TJ was so young, they released him into the custody of his father. Bean and Worm had criminal records, so they got to ride the bus straight to Oak Hill Youth Center in Laurel, Maryland. I had heard a lot of stories about both juvenile jails, especially the one I was in. The average young nigga would've been afraid on his first trip to The Receiving Home, but not me. My life was like a semi empty book, with nothing but a prologue and a dedication page and I was ready to fill it with chapters........

Anthony Fields

Chapter Eight

"The way to be is paradise life relaxing/ black, latino and anglo saxon/ Armani Exchange, deranged/ lost tribe of Shabazz, free at last/ brand new whips to crash as we laugh in the illa path/so many years of depression make vision/ better living/ the type of place to raise kids in/ open their eyes to the lies history's told foul/ cause I'm as wise as the old owl and the gold child..."

"Somebody turn that bamma ass Nas shit off and put some Biggie Smalls on the box.' Michael Hicks announced without looking up from his card game.

Nobody made a move to change the CD in the boombox. After a while, Mike Hicks got up to do it himself. "Since everybody sitting here actin' like didn't nobody hear me, can't nobody touch the box for the rest of the day." He went back to his game. Nobody said a word.

I smiled to myself. Mike Hicks was seventeen years old and somewhat of a professional juvenile prison. He was at the Receiving Home doing juvenile life. I wondered why he wasn't at Oak Hill with all the tough, older niggas. He was taller than most of us and muscular. He was also the bully of the whole juvy jail. Although, I didn't care what was on the radio, I knew that one day, Mike Hicks and I would clash. It was just a matter of time.

That time came two days later. I was sitting at a table with three other dudes playing Spades, when Mike walked up and announced that he wanted to play. When nobody made a move to give up their hand, Mike took the cards that were on the table.

"Aye, joe, you be carrying these niggas in here like straight up bitches and I'm cool with that because it don't

effect me. But now it does when you take the cards that I'm playing spades with. It's like you don't even care about me. Like you saying, 'Fuck me." I'm not these niggas, joe, so can you please put the cards back?"

"Youngin'," Mike Hicks said with a grin, "respect is earned, not given. You haven't earned---"

That was as far as he got as I stood up and leapt on his ass. He outweighed me and was stronger than me, but I was young, fast and focused. Mike Hicks had to grab me to stop my lightening face assault on his body and head.

"Let me go, joe. Why you holding me?" I asked. "Rumble me straight up. Don't hold me."

Mike shoved me back hard and I almost fell. Almost. I regained my footing as he took a fighter's stance in from me. Everybody in the unit crowded around to see the show. And what a show they were in for. I could see from Mike's stance and the way he held his hands that he wasn't a fighter. Everything Damien taught me in and outside of the boxing ring came to me quickly as I *showcased my skills on Mike Hicks. Dizzying combinations of punches. Punches in bunches, Damien called it. By the time the counselors came in to stop the fight, Mike Hicks was in bad shape.*

"Damn, Hicks, you let this young nigga get out on you like that?" Counselor Sheffield asked. "Somebody finally test drove one of them bluff cars you be selling, huh?"

"Fuck you, Sheff. Ain't nobody get out on me. We ain't finished yet." Mike Hicks responded as he pulled away from the counselor that was holding him.

"Keep it up and I'ma let shorty get back on your ass. Keep talking."

"I'm tryna see him again anyway. Let him go."

"Okay," Sheffield said and laughed. "You asked for it. Dawkins let shorty go."

Me and Mike Hicks squared off in front of one another. He stepped in with a straight left jab trying to set me up for a big right hand. But I was hip to his play. I waited patiently until he threw the right hand and overextended himself. He was off balance. I turned to the left and shot a three piece combo at him that dropped him to one knee. Frustrated, he got up and wildly rushed me. I side stepped that, too. Threw an uppercut to the chin and a hook to his body. Mike Hicks dropped again. The counselors had seen enough. They broke up the fight and locked me and Mike in our cells for the rest of the day and all night. Over the next few days, me and Mike fought three more times, all ending the same way. Finally, he accepted the fact that he couldn't fuck with me with hands. After that, my name meant something at the Receiving Home. Everybody catered to me.

Since there were always dudes coming and leaving the Receiving Home, there was no shortage of dudes who wanted to test me. Over the course of about two months, I had maybe ten fights and won them all. While that enhanced my status at the jail, the administrative staff became sick of my shit.

"Fuller, you are too aggressive for my facility." The Director told me one day. "I'm putting your ass on the next thing smoking to Oak Hill."

True to his word, a day later, I was shackled and cuffed and loaded onto a bus. Headed for the next part in the book that was my life.
****

Oak Hill Youth Center was situated over ten acres of land that sat adjacent to the NSA headquarters. There were two barbed wire fences that stood 12 feet tall and encircled the whole grounds. OHYC held all the most aggressive and dangerous juveniles that DC had to offer. New arrivals had to be taking through an intake screening process that required me to be locked in a cell in the intake unit for five days.

On my third day of lockdown, somebody outside my door called my name.

"Lil Redds! Hey, Lil Redds!"

I couldn't see out the door, but I could hear through it. "Yea, what's up? Who that?"

"Here, " Was all I heard before a pack of cigarettes and a baggie of weed was pushed under the door. "That's from Bean. He sends his love."

My day brightened instantly at the mention of Bean's name. I couldn't wait to see my partner again. I turned the jacks and the weed over in my hand and wondered what the hel I was gonna do with it. Bean knew that I didn't smoke or do drugs. "Aye, joe, you still there?" I called out to the dude on the other side of the door.

"I'm here, youngin', what's up?'

"What's your name, joe?"

"Draino. Lil Draino."

"Aight, Draino, let me ask you something. What can I do with all this shit? I don't smoke none of this shit."

"You gotta sell it, joe. These young niggas in here smoke all kinds of shit, especially jacks and weed and ain't nobody in here got none. You can get what you want for it. Money, canteen, whatever. These niggas will give you the shoes off their feet for that tree. They'll give you some ass for the cigarettes. Niggas will give you their food trays if you want that shit. If you don't smoke, that's why Bean sent you that shit. He knows what it go for up here in 10A."

"Will I get to see Bean when I come off lock?"

"Not unless you got an open pop court order."

"Fuck is that?" I asked.

"Fuck is what? A court order?"

"Yeah."

"That's what the judge sends with you here. It tells these muthafuckas how to house you. Everybody in this unit has a Max court order which means they have to stay up here on lockdown. Bean and yall other homie Worm have open pop court orders, so they are in open population. Bean is in 9A and Worm is in 8B."

"I don't know what I got. I was up the Receiving Home and kept fighting and shit so they sent me here, not the judge."

"Either way, you'll find out in a minute. I gotta go, I'ma holla back later, joe."

Two days later, I was let out the cell. In the unit I was in there were two sides to it. 10A and 10B. The other side was for dudes from the compound that had caught a write up. They did a certain amount of days and went back to open pop. I found out that I had to stay in Max for a while until Oak Hill decided I could handle myself in open pop, since I was only twelve years old.

"That's shorty right there." I heard someone say when I walked in the day room.

"Yeah, that's Lil Redd." A dude name Greg added. "Youngin' sharp as shit with hands."

As I looked around the room for any enemy faces, a group of dudes approached me. I was only a hundred and 15 pounds soaking wet and about 5'4. If the whole group brought me a move, I was hit. But one on one, I didn't see anybody that intimidated me in the group.

"Young nigga, what's up?" the lead dude said and stuck out his hand. He was tall and slim with a light brown com- plexion. "I'm Draino. We talked the other day."

My tension faded immediately. "Okay. What's up, joe."

"Ain't shit. Let me introduce my men. This lil curly head dude right here is Chez. That's LA from Galveston, Joe Green, lil Jazz from Congress, my man Really Doe from the Deuce and this is my man Black Venable from Condon Terrace. Your man Bean is my man, joe and everybody down here on the Hill respect him. Since you his man, you are our man. Like a family. Whatever you want or need, we got you. And I'ma help you get off them jacks and shit."

"Aight, cool."

Being at Oak Hill was just like being in the Receiving Home, only a little different. In Oak Hill dudes had weapons. Mop wringers, shanks, sticks, brooms and chemicals to throw in a person's face. There was a lot of violence at Oak Hill but none of it affected me, so I was good. I witnessed dudes who had names in the streets get punked bad in Oak Hill. I saw it all. I saw niggas get robbed. I saw niggas get jumped and stomped. I saw dudes jerk off and cum on dudes faces while they were asleep. After about a month in 10A unit, I was released to open pop. Assigned to unit 7A. I wasn't in the unit twenty whole minutes before the drama started......

Everybody in the day room emptied it to see who was coming in the unit. All eyes were on me as I carried my bed roll to cell 15 in the back hall. My antennas were up and I spotted the SW dudes immediately. There were three of them standing across from the counselor's office. As I walked by, I heard, "That nigga shot my father."

That statement, I knew came from the short dude with the dreads. Mark Harris. Cunta's son. What I had learned while on lock in 10A was that the SW dudes were deep at Oak Hill. They had an alliance with Ridge Road and that made them strong. But they were knee deep in a beef with two other strong neighborhoods. *5th and O Uptown and Condon Terrace. The only reason that SW was even a factor in all the prisons, juvenile and adult, was because of one man. Wayne Perry. DC's most feared killer was born and raised in SW and he loved everyone there. When things got rough, they reached out to Wayne and Wayne left a body cold somewhere to be found. After that understandings would be reached and the SW niggas survived.*

When I walked out of the cell and down the hall, one of the dudes from SW swung on me. He hit me flesh on the corner of my jaw. It hurt, but my frustration made me shake it off. I went at the dude who swung on me with a flurry of punches. He couldn't stand up under the barrage. Then Somebody hit me from behind. Pivoting, I spint around and went at the next dude that turned out to be Mark Harris, the dude that I beat up on Carrollburg street. A couple punches later he was knocked out sleep. "Bitch ass niggas!" I muttered as I stomped Mark in the face with my boots. The other dude was groggy and ready to go, so I focused on him. He covered his head and leaned on the wall like a bitch. I walked over to the other dude that I saw standing with them earlier. "You wanna see me, too, joe?'

"I ain't got nothin' to do with that shit. I'm from Northeast. My grandmother live down the West. You ain't never did nothing to me."

"Next time, nigga, just say naw I ain't tryna see you."

Out of nowhere came another dude. About my height and build, just a little more muscular. He went up to the dude who had just punked out of fighting me and smacked the shit out of him.

"All you bitch niggas make me sick." The newcomer said. "Somebody wake Mark lil sucka ass up." To me, he said, "I'm tryna see you, youngin'. Let's go in the trash room and

work. One of the dudes yall killed was my man."

We went in the trash room and I saw that it was spacious and closed off. It was a good place to fight without being caught by the staff. The dude and I started rumbling immediately after the door was shut. A minute into the fight, I knew that I was in a fight. The dude was good. He slipped, caught, weaved and sidestepped my punches with ease. Suddenly, I was a little worried. I had never faced anybody that was as sharp as me. A dude from Congress Park named Coo-Wop stepped in and stopped the dead even match up.

"Yea, nigga, that's for my homies." The dude I was fighting said.

"You ain't done nothing, joe." I replied." Look at your face."

"Look at your face, nigga. Fuck you talkin' bout."

The dude's words inflamed me. I wasn't used to dudes talking shit to me after a fight. I wanted to—no I needed to whip his ass. "You talk a good one, joe. C'mon, let's finish."

The dude snatched away from Coo-Wop. "You heard the man. He said we ain't finished yet."

Anger made me quicker, sharper, meaner. After a couple minutes, my opponent was a little overwhelmed. My fight game was superior to his and he was starting to realize that. The determined, yet defeated look in his eyes were priceless. His heart was big, but his wind was short. The dude gassed out and Wop broke up the fight for a second time.

"That's it, joe. You had enough." Wop told the dude. "Live to fight another day."

The dude accepted defeat. Quietly he walked away.

"Slim is a soldier, Redds. You gotta respect him. He fought a good fight and lost. A rack of these niggas around here won't even do that. He rumbled your homies Worm and Bean when they first got here."

"What happened?"

"Happened with what?"

"Bean and worm when they fought that dude."

"Oh, he whipped Bean and Worm. We had to beg Bean not to stab him though. You know Bean shit lunchin'. He didn't take that lost too well. You the only one who ever beat shorty in a fight."

"I'm a see him again when he get hisself together."

"Yeah, yall gon definitely have to work again, but that's later. For right now, let's get you settled in and then we'll go outside later, so you can see Bean and Worm."

"Fuck Worm, joe. That nigga wicked."

"I heard."

"Aye, the dude I was fighting, what's his name?"

"Cutty. They call him Cutty."

****

"What your lawyer talkin bout?" Bean asked me.

"I haven't seen no lawyer since we first came in," I told him.

"Your lawyer some shit, young. Mines said that the case is weak as shit. We ain't even been indicted yet. It's been 3 months."

"It don't even matter to me, joe." I said. *"It's whatever."*

"Nigga, you lunching like shit," Devon opined. *"Juvenile life ain't no joke. You'll be in this bamma ass joint until you 21. Fuck all that. I'm tryna get out there to the bitches."*

"Wild nigga, you ain't got shit but a distribution. You ain't facing no time. You out there stealing cars and selling coke. How you gone be a car thief and a hustler? That shit don't mix," Bean joked. We all laughed. *"You better be lucky your ass ain't on the beef with us."*

"Yea, nigga, you got me down here for nothing and I wasn't even with yall that night. Ya'll need to tell them people something and let me go." Worm added.

As we always did on the street, we ignored Worm. After a while, he walked away from us.

"Lucky ass nigga got away," Bean said to Devon, who had only come to Oak Hill a few days ago. "I can't catch a break."

"Slim," I said animated, "did you hear that nigga Worm when the cops had us on the fence in front of Esha house?"

Bean looked at me and smiled. "Of course, I heard that punk ass nigga."

"He was dry snitching like a mutherfucka. Talkin 'bout, 'I ain't do nothing, you better holla at them niggas.' Joe, that nigga would've pointed us out if his hands wouldn't have been cuffed behind his back."

"That nigga always been a bitch," Devon said.

"I ain't even tryna keep talkin 'bout that nigga. Ya'll still got jacks?"

"I'm out," I said.

"Me too," Devon added.

Bean reached into his waistband and produced two packs of Newport cigarettes, two dub bags of weed and a roll of money. He gave me and Devon a pack of cigarettes and a bag of weed. The money he handed to me.

"Where my street money at nigga?" Devon complained.

"Shut the fuck up, nigga. That's Redds shit. Damien sent that to him through my counselor connect," Bean told Devon. To me, he said, "Damien sends his love to you and said to tell you that he been hearing about you."

All I could do was smile. Damien Lucas's compliment went a long way with me.

"You been talking to anybody around the way on the

phone ?" Bean asked.

"Nobody but Kemie and Esha."

"Man, somebody told me that you said you fucked Esha. Did you?" Devon asked

"Naw, joe. We like sister and brother," I lied.

"Yeah, nigga, whatever. You ain't fuck Kemie yet?"

"Naw. She told me she ain't fuckin until she turn 16."

"Aye, slim, I'ma tell you who pussy is good as a mutha-fucka," Bean said.

"Who?" I asked.

"Dawn. Her shit a snapper joint. All of it."

I laughed real hard. "Creep ass nigga, her pussy is sup-posed to be good. Dawn is my age, if not younger than me," I laughed. "Chester molester ass nigga."

"Nigga, fuck you," Bean laughed..

"Naw, nigga. Fuck with me," I replied and shot a jab at him.

Bean rushed me and bear hugged me. I'ma put them hot balls in your lil ass. Keep it up."

I tried to get out of his embrace. He kissed my head.

"I love yall niggas, joe. Straight up."

"I love you, too, joe."

Anthony Fields

Chapter Nine

"Your honor, we actively pursued witness to testify against the defendants during this investigation. We were unsuccessful at doing so. So at this time, we have no other recourse, but to dismiss the murder charges against the defendants."

"Verbal motion to dismiss is granted. The defendants are free to go."

Outside the courtroom it seemed like the whole neighborhood was there to welcome us home. It felt good to be free. It was the summer of 1995 and I was now thirteen years old.

"Damn, your lil ass gained some weight while you were gone. Grew a few inches, too." Bay One said as she hugged me.

"Nine months in juvey will do that to a person, Bay. How you been?"

"I'm good, Lil Redds. Where you about to go?"

"Over Kemie house." I told her. *"I'ma see you and Esh later."*

"You know I need some pussy, Kemie. I beel locked up almost a year. Feel my dick." I grabbed Kemie's hand and placed it on my hard dick. When I moved my hand and Kemie's lingered there I thought that I had her where I wanted her. I unzipped my shorts and pulled my dick out. *"Look at all the precum I'm drippin'."*

"Boy, look how big your thing is. Ain't no way all that is gonna fit in me. Not gon happen."

"Not gon happen? Not gon happen? Kemie you can't be serious."

Kemie stared at my dick and said, "Dead serious."

"C'mon, Kemie, I swear to God, I'ma be gentle with you. Don't you love me?"

"Of course, I do. Haven't I always shown you that? I wrote you and sent you pictures while you were locked up. What other 12 year old would do that? But writing is one thing, letting you break me in is another. You gotta wait, Redds. Until I'm 16. I already told you that. Besides, I heard that you was having sex with Esha before you went to jail. Go around the corner and hump on her."

"Hump Esha? Are you serious? You believe that stuff that people be saying around here?"

"Why shouldn't I believe it?"

"Because Esha is like a sister to me. That's why."

"Yeah, whatever."

"So, I can't get no pussy?"

"Not until I turn 16."

"I'ma have blue balls by then. I'm outta here. Call you later."

"Why you actin' like that?" Kemie shouted. "Where you going at?"

Kemie's questions went unanswered. I was out the door and walking up the street.

****

"While you two were in, we had to do some major politicking to make sure that none of them niggas from down the West came to court on yall." Creeko inform me and Bean as we sat in my uncle's apartment around Capers. Marquette sat in a lazy boy recliner eating apple and TJ played video games on the floor. "I had to put a few dollars out there and a little bit of Coke, but them niggas kept their end of the deal. I don't know how they tryna carry it though. According to

Vito Hill, yall didn't kill anybody but some nobodies. They say the shit is squashed and they ain't   trippin'. But I don't believe that. I think they tryna rock us to sleep. So, yall just keep yall heads up."

"Where my hammer at?" Bean asked.

"Still at Bay One house where you left it. All of yall joints are there."

"I'm about to go and get my joint." Bean said and left.

"Thanks for everything, joe." I told Creeko as I shook his hand. I rose to follow Bean out the door, but Damien stopped me.

"Did you get all the shit I sent you every month? The money? Everything?"

"Yea, I did. Thanks, Dee. I appreciated that shit like a muthafucka. I would've been fucked up if it wasn't for you."

"That shit ain't shit. All I did was what was supposed to be done." Damien said and cut his eyes over to Marquette. "If I wouldn't have done it, nobody was gonna do it. Ain't that right, Quette?"

"Huh? What you say?"

"Exactly." Damien muttered under his breath. "You was about to go and get your gun, wasn't you?"

I nodded my head.

"Fuck that joint, youngin'. That joint hot as hell now. Let somebody else fight over that joint. I got some new shit for you."

TJ looked up from the video game. "I wasn't ear hustling, but I heard what you just said Damien. Can I have the nine if Redds ain't gon need it?"

"It's yours, youngin'. Go get it from Bay One's house."
TJ rushed out the house. "C'mon, Redds, you going with me."

In Damien's new BMW wagon, he passed me a chrome handgun. It barely fit into my palm.

"That's yours, youngin'. It's a Springfield Armory Colt .45. Holds 6 in the clip and one in the head. The kick-back is powerful. You gotta be strong when you bust it. You look like you done gain a little muscle since you been in. I think you gon be okay with it. Now, them SW niggas are sneaky. Especially the young niggas like Pimp, Chin, Draper, Meechie, Poo Poo, Raymond Washington, Ericky Berk, Sean Birdie and all them niggas. They gon try and creep you. Keep the fifth on you at all times and I got some fully shit that I'ma give you, too. Don't let none of these niggas out here kill you. You hear me?"

"I hear you, joe. Loud and clear. Fuck them niggas. I'll kill all them niggas, Dee. Today."

"I already know, youngin'. I already know. Another thing.....if you gon start back fucking Esha, strap up and don't catch feelings. The pussy good and all that, I know, but don't fall in lo---"

"I never fucked Esh---"

"You ain't gotta lie to me. She told me already. Right after I fucked her." Damien looked me in the eyes to read my expression. My face was a mask. My emotion hidden. "The SW beef aside, I got some good news for you."

"Oh yea? What?"

"While you were away, this dude surfaced. I know who he is, but I want you to see if you recognize him."

"Who is he?"

Damien turned the corner onto K street. "You'll see, He's gonna be outside on Tracy's porch."

We rode down the street until I spotted a crowd of dudes standing in front of a house.

"The dude right there in the blue jeans, grey shirt----"

"Rick! That's the dude Rick that killed my mother! I can't believe it! Stop the car, joe!"

"Not right now, youngin'."

I suddenly got very upset. Tears welled up in my eyes. I turned to Damien and exploded."Fuck you mean, not right now?! I'ma crush his ass out here in front of everybody. Stop the car and let me out!" Damien ignored me and kept driving. Tears fell down my face as my anger and hate spilled over inside me. "Let me out, Dee!"

Around the corner, Damien stopped the car. I went for the door, but he reached over and grabbed my arm. I pulled away, but his grip was solid. Like iron. "Listen, young nigga! Don't you think I know how bad you wanna kill that nigga right now?! I wanted to kill him myself when I saw him the other day. But I couldn't rob you of your revenge. Your destiny. This bitch nigga gon just come back around here like shit sweet. I want you to roast his ass. But not right now. Use your head, youngin'. You just came home. It ain't been 24 hours yet and you about to go back on another body. Naw. That ain't smart. I know you're still learning and all that, but youngin', listen to me. You gotta do shit and get away with it. Feel me? Plus, what you don't know, can't see is that one of the dudes in the crowd around there was an off duty police nigga named Mike Day. You go and crush him right this minute and you going back to jail for sure. If that's what you want—" Damien let my shirt go. "Go 'head then. Do it. And after that, I'm through fuckin' with you. Your choice. Go or stay. What you gonna do?"

My anger subsided a little. Damien's words penetrated my core. Breathing in deeply, I said, "You right. I'ma chill out for right now, but I'm definitely killing that bitch nigga soon."

"I respect that. You gon get him. Trust and believe that.

The element of surprise is on your side. He don't have a clue that you about to hop on his line."

"But he will know soon. That's on my mother's grave."

The next day, I couldn't wait any longer. I couldn't sleep, eat or focus. I kept seeing Rick's face, then and now. I kept seeing him beat my mother as she begged for her life. I saw him dying by my hand. Me watching as the holes opened up in his face, blood coming out until his heart stopped pumping it. With my black wave cap on my head, I walked around the corner to where Rick was the day before. Damien told me that Rick was there everyday. I saw Rick as soon as I hit the sidewalk. He walked up to me. I lowered my head. Rick walked past me, oblivious to my presence or identity. Letting him get around the corner and up the street was a planned move by me. I didn't want him in front of the house on K street. As inconspicuously as I possibly could, I followed Rick. He walked into a building not too far from the one I grew up in. I watched as he disappeared inside the building. "Don't be in there too long, joe. Come back quick and let me kill you slow."

Standing out on the sidewalk suddenly seemed like a bad idea to me and I looked around for cover. The only thing that I saw was the big green dumpster on the side of the building. Without much thought, I climbed into the dumpster, sat on some trash and waited. The dumpster wasn't even half full and it stunk like hell. Different smells assaulted my nostrils immediately and I had to hold back an urge to hurl. Then I thought back to when I was seven and standing in the closet ignoring the smell of my own bodily waste and the smell of my mother's rotting corpse. About an hour later, Rick emerged from the building. Quickly, but quietly, I climbed out of the dumpster. I walked behind Rick. The .45 hidden beside my leg. Whatever was in Rick's hand was important to him because it had all of his attention. Good for me, bad for him. By the time he heard my approach it was too late. He turned and stared at me as I raised the gun as if in slow motion. I watched his eyes grow large. They locked on mine. Suddenly I was transported back in time and Rick was wearing jeans and a t-shirt. Beating and kicking my mother.

Boom! Boom! The cannon in my hand roared twice before I had to use my other hand to steady my aim. I watched rick's body drop and him squirm all over the pavement. He hollered and begged for his life. I walked right up and stood over him.

"Please don't kill me! What did I do? What did I do?"

"That's funny. My mother asked yall not to kill her, just like you're doing now. It didn't work for her and it won't work for you."

I fired round after round from the powerful handgun until it was empty. Quarter size holes made Rick look as if he was real. But he was dead. All the way dead. I smiled as I walked away.

Anthony Fields

Chapter Ten

"Boy, I ain't fuckin' with you."

Ignoring what her mouth was saying, I continued to caress her as she leaned on the counter in the kitchen.

"Stop, Redds! I just told you that I ain't fuckin' with you like that."

"Why not? What I do?" I asked.

"For one, I told your ass not to tell nobody that we was fuckin' and you did. And two, you out here killing people. That's why not."

"I ain't killing nobody. Whoever told you that, they lying."

"Is that right? And they lying about you telling people we been fuckin', too, huh?"

"Yea, they lying. Did they tell you that people said I told them you sucked my dick?"

"Naw, haven't heard that one. I bet not hear that one."

"Aight then, if I had told niggas that we fucking, don't it make better sense that I would also tell them you eating my dick?"

"Boy, what the fuck ever. Eating your dick....you lil ass getting to big for your britches. And everybody know you killed Rick for what he did to your mother. Admit it."

"Admit it? Who you? The police? I ain't done shit." I said, grabbed Esha and turned her around. "I got something for you to tell people though."

"And what's that, Redds?"

"This." I bent Esha over and ate her pussy from the back.

****

Three months later, two days before Thanksgiving, I saw the second dude involved in my mother's death. He looked exactly the same but a little stockier. He was dressed in a grey All Daz 24/7 sweatsuit and 991 New Balance running shoes. His hair was cut low and perfectly tapered. My eyes followed his every move as he walked up to a female standing on a porch and talked to her. The gun in my waist got heavy. I was ready to lighten it's load. Minutes later, the couple headed to a burgundy Nissan Maxima.

"Aye, Bean, where your dirt bike at?" I tapped Bean's shoulder and asked. He was down on his knees gambling.

"Parked in Wayne Wayne court. Why?"

"I need you to do me a favor right quick."

"What's up?"

"Put the dice down and go with me."

We caught up to the Maxima as it idled at the light on Eight Street. Bean wore a helmet. I didn't. In broad daylight as traffic moved up and down the street, I hopped off the bike and ran up to the passenger side of the Maxima. Moody's eyes grew large as the recognition set in. I upped the gun and fired into the car window. He attempted to duck, but his attempts were futile. I walked up to the window and made sure that I blew his brains out. The woman in the driver's seat screamed.

"Bitch stop all that screaming before I kill your ass." I told the female before walking, not riding on the bike with Bean, back to the hood.

****

"Nigga, what the fuck is wrong with you?" Marquette exploded as soon as he pulled over and hopped out of his Ford Bronco.

Me, Bean, TJ, PeeWee, Tubby, and Bowlegged Dion were shooting dice on C Street. I looked up at my uncle and paid him no mind.

He walked up and grabbed me by my Polo shirt. "I know you heard me, Redds? What the fuck are you lunching off of?"

I snatched my shirt from his grasp. "Fuck off me, joe." I said and picked up the dice. "Who got me? I'm shooting fifty." The next thing I know I was blind-sided by a punch. It was a good solid punch that knocked me onto my butt and hands. I was dazed like hell.

"Go 'head with that shit 'Quette." Bean said and stood up.

"Nigga you better mind your business." Marquette spat at Bean.

"He is my business, joe and that ain't cool with you just did. Don't do that shit no more." Bean stated.

"Or what? Or what, Bean?" Marquette said challenging Bean.

Bean walked over to me and helped me to my feet. I brushed off my clothes. I had tears in my eyes and venom rushing through my blood. I heard the roar of the beast.

"You gon make a nigga bust your bitch ass, Quette. No bullshit. Keep it up." Bean told Quette. "The only reason you ain't already got it is because I'm the family.

"I ain't tryna hear that shit." Quette said to Bean, then he turned to me and said, "You getting too big for your britches, nephew. You ain't grown yet. Don't never disrespect me in front of these niggas."

"Aye, Unc," I said with a renewed sense of calm, but with a deadly tone, "if you ever do that again, I'ma...

"You gon what? Do I look scared of you nigga? You got these niggas scared of you because you shooting and killing niggas in the street. That shit ain't proper. You tryna go to prison for the rest of your stupid ass life? You outta control, slim.

"Outta control? I'm outta control because I crushed two niggas that killed my mother? That was your sister, joe! Fuck you talking 'bout! I just did what the fuck you supposed to did six years ago. You let them niggas kill your sister and you knew who they were because I told you. I told you. I told you it was Rick and Moody and what did you do? Nothing;

After them niggas killed my mother, I heard the nigga Moody tell Rick that Margie was your sister and guess what he said?

He said, fuck that young nigga. He don't want it with me. And he was right. That's what I thought about when I nailed his ass to the ground. I did that. I nailed his ass to the ground and I just put that nigga Moody brains all over that lil' ass Nissan he was in;

I did that. Not you. So miss me with all the dramatic shit. Talkin' bout, I'm outta control' for my family and for my men, I' ma stay outta control. I do me. I didn't ask you for shit. You ain't never laced my boots up about nothing. So, don't try to tell me what to do. My father work in a barbershop for a living and I didn't even listen to him;

You ain't gotta like what I do, but you gotta respect me, slim. You can't be walking up sucker punching a nigga and shit. That's out. Make that your last time for that, or I' ma forget you my uncle. That's on my mama grave."

My uncle lowered his head and just walked away.

****

"After that everybody just started calling me Dirty Redds." I told Umar. "Because I was out there crushing shit and doing niggas dirty the way I was getting at them."

"You told me that at the beginning of the story, slim."

Umar said.

"Well, I'm telling you again. It was worth noting, cuz. Don't you think?"

"And here I was thinking they called you Dirty Redds because you didn't like taking bathes. Sorta like the way you are now."

"Whatever, cuz. You know I'm part dolphin. I stay in that water."

"On some real live shit, though slim. I respect how you knocked them two niggas off that killed Moms. That was gangsta. I would've done the same thing."

"Cuz, you faking. You wouldn't have opened them niggas shit up like me. I like to see that brains and shit hanging out. I like when the blood and bone and brains be all mixed in together looking like jello and shit. All my shit be head and face shit. I be knocking the nose and lips and shit off niggas."

"Slim, you sick. On some real live sadistic sick, Hannibal Lector type sick. I done crushed me a few niggas, too, but it don't matter how I kill them. Two to the chest. One in the back. It don't matter."

"Well, it matters to me. I wanna make sure you dead. I told you what the big homie Damien told me that day. Get up on a nigga and hit 'em. Make sure he's dead. I ain't never left a survivor, cuz. Never."

Umar hopped off the top bunk and went to the sink. "I'ma make wudu and then we gotta get the Mahgrib in. Then you can tell me some more about Esha and Kemie and the rest of the hood."

"That's a bet, cuz. That's a bet."

****

"After my fallout with my uncle, I started really wildin' out. I was 13 going on 30 in my mind and couldn't nobody tell me shit. The shit I was doing with Esha kinda just tapered off and then stopped. We just naturally got back on some platonic, homie shit. I wasn't mad though because my name was raging so much, all the young chicks wanted to find out what was happening with me..."

"So you're Dirty Redds, huh?" the pretty brown skinned girl with the long braids asked.

I checked her out and liked what I saw. She looked like a young Janet Jackson in the movie Poetic Justice. "Yeah, that's me. Who are you?"

"I'm Mildred."

"Mildred? Shit, I heard of you. You from 7th Street, right? But up near the private homes. Where Mark Raphen office at."

"I'm right across the street from Mark. What have you heard about me?"

"What have you heard about me?"

"You can't keep answering a question with a question."

"Says who? I play by my own set of rules."

"So, I heard. How old are you, Redds?"

"Fourteen. Why? How old do you want me to be?"

"I at least thought you was Bean and 'em age. You are too young for me." Mildred said.

"A'ight, then, I'm out." I said and turned to leave.

Mildred stopped me. "I didn't say leave. I just said you was young. I like your freckles and you're cute as shit. Walk with me somewhere."

I gripped the gun in my waist. I felt secure. "Let's go."

****

"A-a-a-r-r-gh shit! Yes! Fuck me! Fuck me!" Mildred called out. "Fuck this pussy nigga! Fuck it! Harder! Harder! Shit! That's it! Like that! Hard like that!"

I had just met Mildred twenty minutes ago and there I was in her bed, naked with both of her pretty feet on my shoulders. And she made me put them there, it was called the "Buck" she told me. The way Mildred moaned, groaned and talked during sex was insane. I fucked Mildred for hours and everything that I hadn't learned from Esha, I learned from Mildred that day. She never did tell me what she'd heard about me, but I was glad that she heard it. What I learned about Mildred was that she was fucking with no lame niggas. She loved thugs, hustlers, killers, and gorillas. And to her I embodied them all.

Mildred was a cold blooded freak and loved it. Over the next few days, she had me eating her pussy in all different positions, tonguing her ass, and licking her toes. She even gave me some ass. She wanted me to hit her in the ass while she bent over, but I had other plans. I put her on the bed on her side, the same way Marquette did Tosca that day I watched. I wanted to see if she made the same faces as Tosca. And since there was a floor to ceiling length on her closet door, I got the chance to see Mildred's face as she took that dick in her backdoor. She made the same faces as Tosca and that made me cum in her ass way faster than I wanted too.

My relationship with Mildred, I can't really define. She was four years older than me and had other niggas that she fucked with. Niggas that I knew she was fucking, but I didn't even care. As long as she gave me the pussy, I was good. Mildred was the woman that simplified things for me and turned me on to new shit. The money that she got from other niggas she spent on me.

Mildred introduced me to Solbiato, Armani, Exchange,

Hugo Boss, and Gucci. She took me shopping at Tyson's Corner and Mezza's Galleria. Mildred was the one that showed me life outside of Capers projects. While everybody else my age was at Wild World and Kings Dominion, Mildred had me at the beach in Ocean City and riding jet skis on Myrtle Beach in South Carolina, to Mildred, I wasn't a manchild, I was a man.

Then tragedy struck. Mildred and two of her friends. Shampoo and Donnika were at a nigga house in Bowie when some other niggas invaded the house to rob it. The dudes killed two dudes, including the dude who owned the house, and Mildred. Word was that Mildred and the two dudes went for guns to shoot it out. They didn't make it. That situation fucked me up and made me turn to alcohol and weed.

I didn't understand life at all. I questioned why I was even born. I wondered why God would do a lot of the things that I thought he did. The only thing that I did understand was that everybody living was born to die. In one way or another, all we had coming for sure was a chance to die. Once that irrefutable fret was cemented in my brain, I decided that I wanted to control how I died. I had to go out like an outlaw. Guns blazing. I wanted a gangsta's death.

****

"Stop it, Redds! Stop!" Kemie screamed. "You're drunk! Stop it! Get off of me!"

I paid Kemie no mind as I pinned her to the wall in her bedroom trying to pull her jeans down. She struggled against me determined to keep her pants up. "I'm not drunk."

"You must be if you think you gon rape me. Stop it, Redds. Stop! Stop!"

Kissing all over her neck, I told Kemie, "I'm just tryna

get some love from my girl."

"It's not time, yet, Redds. Stop it! Damn, you can't wait 10 more months?"

"Why should I have too?" I asked letting Kemie go.

"Good question, nigga. With all the bitches you fucking around here, you shouldn't need no more pussy. Especially not mine."

"Man, you trippin!"

"Naw, nigga, you trippin'. Getting your dick sucked by crackhead bitches and dope fiends and shit. You think I don't know about all the wicked shit you be on? Well, I do. The streets be talking, Redds and I be listening."

I sat down on Kemie's bed and laid back. My head was starting to pound. "Go head, joe, you blowing me now."

"I'm blowing you? Naw, I ain't blowing you and that's why you mad. In here tryna take the pussy. You not getting none from me until I want to, so you go right ahead and stick your dick in all them other bitches mouths. Because you won't put it in mine. Your little dirty dick is ass. You make me sick, boy. Actin' all pissed and shit."

"Ain't never been pressed, Kemie. About nothing and nobody."

"I can't tell Redds. You gotta be pressed to bust a nut if you out here in the streets fucking them nasty ass crackheads. You had the nerve to trick with Darlene, Redds. And you know that that's Jay Jay's mother. How could you do that to him? He be outside with y' all and you trickin' his mother. That's fucked up. You fucked up. You wild as shit."

I'd heard enough. I was ready to bounce. But before I did, I said, "You're right, Kemie. And everything you just called me is true. But that's who I am. The problem is that you are the only person in my life that hadn't realized that yet. Did you know that you are the only person that still calls me

Redds? I haven't been Redds for years, Kemie. Redds died with them dudes that killed my mother. I'm Dirty Redds now. I been him for about two years now and you haven't opened your eyes up large enough to see the new me. I'm fucked in the head and heart, Kemie. I'm foul. I'm wild. I'ma young nigga that thrive off the street life. I enjoy gambling and killing. That's who I am, Kemie. You can't see that because you are caught up in school, your family, and your friends. Me, what do I love, Kemie? Huh? I got my men, some guns, and my bitch, a pitbull named Charmin. That's what I got, Kemie."

Tears were in Kemie's eyes. The hurt look on her face left me unfazed, though.

"That's not true. You have me."

"Do I?" I asked, turned and left her house.

****

"Man, that's fucked up how they did big boy." Bean remarked.

I pulled my beeper off my hip and glared at the number on it. "Big Boy, who?"

"Biggie Smalls. Them California niggas killed big boy yesterday."

Notorious BIG was one of my favorite rappers and his death was a blow to the whole state of hip hop. "You bullshittin', joe. Biggie ain't dead."

"Nigga, where you been at? That shit been on the news for 27 hours straight. He was out Cali promoting his new CD and somebody smoked his ass. I guess they really think he had something to do with Tupac getting killed.

All I could do was shake my head. Niggas couldn't even rap and get money without getting smoked. That shit was crazy for real. When Tupac got killed the year before, I wasn't surprised because that nigga was trying to live the life he was rapping about, raping bitches, shooting police, and shit like that. He was beefing with the whole rap industry, so his death came as no shock to me. But hearing that Biggie Smalls was now dead, that fucked me up. "That's fucked up, joe. No bullshit."

"Speaking of rap niggas," Tee said, "that nigga Scarface is at the Ritz tonight with Rare Essence. Y' all tryna go through there? I am."

"Yeah, that's what's up." Bean replied.

"I'm there." Wayne Wayne said.

"Count me in. I need to see Essence. I haven't partied with the sisters in months. I gotta fit already and everything." Omar added.

I looked at my homie Tee and noticed that he had been outside around us every day lately and that wasn't usually him. He was used to getting money in a few different hoods and we were barely seeing him. Then I looked around and didn't see his truck. Tee had one of them new Chevy Tahoe joints and it was always parked somewhere near him. "Tee, where your truck at, joe?" I asked.

"I-I-put it up." Tee replied. "I'ma cop me something new in a minute. Maybe that new Range Rover."

"Okay, then. That's what's up. Get money."

A few minutes later, Tee walked away and everybody laughed. I wondered why. It didn't take me long to find out.

"Man, you hear that nigga?" Bean asked Wayne Wayne.

"Yeah, I heard him. Wellin' ass nigga." Wayne Wayne responded.

Devan looked at me and said, "Tee broke as shit, slim and he think that don't nobody know about it. He went up New York with some niggas thinking they was cool and shit.

Took a hundred and something grand up there to buy some water and them niggas robbed his dumb ass. He had to call Bay One to come and get him. He didn't even have enough money to get back home. He been out here on the block selling dope. They say Creeko had to put him back on his feet, fronted a dipper of dope."

"Aye, slim," T.J. said, "That nigga might be blowing that shit, too. I saw him in the oil joint last night with Pinky and nem. Y' all know what Pinky and Tish nem be doing, fuck he hanging with them for?"

"He probably tricking them trifling ass bitches." Bean said.

My beeper went off again. Again it was Kemie's number displayed the screen. And again, I ignored it. "So we going to see Essence tonight, huh?"

****

"Slim, they crankin' like shit." I whispered to Bean over the din of the loud go-go music. People were everywhere in the Ritz, the club was packed. The crowd was probably 60% female and they were dancing hard and coming out of their clothes.

"Them Langston Lane niggas should be smiling." The lead rapper Whiteboy called out to the crowd. "You know why?"

"Why?" the crowd hollered back.

"Because Angie and Tonya ain't got no drawers on, on, on…them Congress Park niggas should be smiling…you know why? Cause Moochie and Yoni ain't got no drawers on, on. All them Capers Niggas should be smiling…you know why? Because Marnie and Reesie ain't got no drawers on…"

I was chilling having a good time, but as always when you live in a city like DC, something is bound to happen.

"C'mon, let's go!" Bean grabbed my shoulder and said. "I think that's Devan and nem over there about to get into with them Potomac Gardens niggas. Let's go and see."

We moved through the crowd with alacrity and force. By the time we got to the crowd that gathered around our homie, I just swung at the first face that I saw that wasn't with us. I knocked that dude out and moved on to the next dude. Bean, Tee, Wayne Wayne and the rest of my homies were also fighting dudes. The club's security rushed the whole scene and broke up the fights.

Everybody rushed for the exits. Nobody wanted to be the ones coming out of the club and your new enemies were already outside. Everybody in the club knew what came next. Gun play. And we didn't disappoint. We ran to our cars and got our guns and went back to the Ritz. The Potomac Gardens dudes did the same. On sight we started shooting at one another. When the police showed up, everybody scattered.

Back around the way, everybody gathered in Wayne Wayne's court, in front of his building. All of us were accounted for and untouched.

"What the fuck happened?" Bean asked Devan.

"Them bitch ass niggas was deep as shit, parying with them 15th and Compton niggas. Yo' when them niggas get twisted and deep that's a cocktail made for starting shit. The nigga Ron Ron be sicing them niggas up. Troy and Lil James got to wilding out, dancing all hard when Essence shouted them out. Bamma ass niggas almost knocked me down. I said something to Troy and that's when shit hit the fan."

"That must be when I looked over there and saw y'all in each other's faces. I grabbed Dirty Redds and we rushed over. I knocked out like two of them niggas. Them niggas was bullshittin'. They know…"

KOK-KOK-KOK-KOK-KOK-KOK-KOK…

BOCKA-BOCKA-BOCKA…

BOOM-BOOM-BOOM-BOOM…

"What the fuck?" I muttered as I ran for cover in the building.

"I'm hit, moe! I'm hit!" Devan announced. "I can't feel nothing, moe!"

The shooting outside the building stopped. I waited a minute before leaving out to check on the rest of my men. They were safe and walking back to the building. "Devan is hit. He's in the hallway leaking like shit." I told Bean and Tee.

"Let's get him to my car and take him to the hospital." Wayne Wayne said.

We went in the building and lifted Devan. We took him to Wayne's Cadillac Eldorado and put him in the back seat.

"You take him and we gon' stay here." Bean said. Wayne Wayne nodded and pulled off. "I guess I ain't gotta tell y' all who that was, right?"

I was high off the weed and pissed off. A fired burned in my eyes and I could hear the roars of the beast inside me. "And I guess I don't have to tell y' all what I'm about to do, right?" I replied calmly.

"Aw shit. Here we go." Tee replied and smiled.

"Bean, you gotta take me to get the bitch."

"The bitch? You gon' take the Pitbull with us?" Bean asked.

"Naw, joe, the other bitch. Andrea Romenski."

"Oh, the AR-15? You gon pull her out for this?"

"Why not? I'ma fuck them niggas up. They could've just smoked my shit out here. They didn't. That's their fault. I'ma spank their asses and let 'em know they been bad. Real bad."

****

"Ain't that them right there?" I asked, as I skulked low in the bushes around the Gardens.

Bean looked in the direction I pointed. "That looks like Derron, Ant John, Gunz, Breeze, Scoop, and Bill."

Potomac Gardens was a labyrinth of low rise tenements and apartment buildings. You couldn't just drive down a street and open fire on them like they did us, so we had to walk in with our guns. "Over there across from them is Marcus, Antonio, Short Short, and Ron Ron. Which ones do you wanna get?"

Bean had an 8 short Mossberg pump and two nine millimeters." He shrugged, "fuck it. Let's get 'em all. You take the big group; I'll take the small one."

"Let's do it, joe." I said and crept out of the bushes. As soon as Bean let the pump go, I let the AR go. The AR cut down everything in its path, but dudes still were able to flee. Well not all of them. As I ran up to where the crowd was just standing, four of the six dudes was gone. Only Ant John and Bill remained. Half of Bill's head was already missing so I stepped over him and stood over Ant John. I could hear Bean now firing the handguns.

"Dirty Redds, slim, it wasn't me. I swear, slim. It wasn't me." Ant John pleaded. "Don't kill me, slim. I ain't even do shit."

"Who did it, then? Who came through Capers shooting just now?"

"That was Troy and them 15th Street niggas. He mad cause one of y' all knocked him out at the go-go."

I aimed the AR and fired, hitting Ant John right in the head. Then I ran the way we'd come, meeting Bean back at the car.

"What now?" Bean asked me the way he always did after we put in work.

"15th Street. Troy Richardson's hot faggie ass brought 15th Street niggas through the hood."

****

"What's up with Derron?" I asked Tubby, the first nigga I saw.

"He got hit in the back and in the leg, but they say he gon' be a'ight."

"That's what's up." I replied and kept it moving. Tubby was my homie that always had an opinion about something, but didn't never want to do nothing. So I avoided, him much as possible.

I walked down towards Esha and saw Omar, PeeWee, and my uncle Marquette standing outside.

"What's up, nephew?" Marquette said.

"Ain't shit, unc. I'm chilling." I replied.

"Where Bean at?" Omar asked me.

"In the house still sleep. Why? What's up?"

"Sop Sop and nem just came through here talking 'bout we killed three of their men up the Gardens last night. He told Creeko that it's about to be a long hot summer."

"So?" I asked starting to get a little irritated.

"You don't get it, do you? It's winter time. He tryna say that; that hot shit gon be flying down here so much, it's gon' feel like summer."

"And?"

"Y' all went through the Gardens and killed three niggas and them niggas hood three blocks from us. Three nigga..."

"Five. We killed five niggas. Three around the Gardens and two on 15th Street. And their hood is about six blocks from us, but I'm failing to understand your point, O. Spit it out. Say whatever you tryna say in ten words or less, because I'm getting mad, slim. No bullshit."

"Slim, who the fuck do you really think you is? You bout to have the whole hood beefing with…"

I whipped out my four fifth and shot Omar in the leg. Boom!

"Ooow- owww- he shot me! He shot me!" Omar rolled around on the ground saying, while holding onto his injured leg.

"That's who the fuck I am, you bitch ass nigga. The nigga that just shot you in the leg. Coward ass nigga. We put that work in for Devan, nigga. We did that shit for him. We didn't know how bad he was hit and whether or not he was gon make it. Them niggas came through here and shot at us. They started it, we continued it. If they wanna make the winter seem like summer, fuck it. Let's get it on. You let that nigga Sop Sop come down here and spook your scared ass. He couldn't have never threatened me like that and walked away from here. I'd have smashed his ass right here. Then asked whoever was with him, what's next? You better stick to stealing cars and leave this gangsta shit to the gangstas."

"Call an ambulance! I'm bleeding to death." Omar hollered.

"Fuck you nigga. Go steal one. You kleptomaniac ass nigga. I still remember how shook you was back in the day when we went and gun at them Southwest niggas."

"Dirty Redds, ease up, youngin. You wrong, slim." Pee Wee said.

I turned to face him. "How the fuck am I wrong? This nigga started that shit. I finished it." I looked at my uncle, who I expected to say something, but he didn't say a word. Calming down, I watched Pee Wee help Omar up off the ground and walked him into Esha's house. I looked at my uncle and said "Stay on point out here, unc. And dress warm because Sop Sop said it's about to be summer. Fuck them niggas."

****

Somebody ended up putting the police on me. That's what happened next. The police snatched me and Bean up and questioned us about all five of the recent murders. We never talked and they sent me back to Oak Hill and Bean over to the juvenile block at D.C. jail. When I got to Oak Hill, I was told that Chez and the rest of my old crew was gone. Either to the streets or to the compound. Looking out my cell door window, I looked for a friendly face and saw none.

I smiled to myself. Things were about to get interesting. After my five-day intake lockdown, I came out of the cell and peeped the scene in the day room. Then I checked out the seating order in the TV area. Again I smiled. I went to the back of the day room, found a deck of cards and started doing push-ups. About thirty minutes into my workout, the games began.

"Aye, moe," one of two dudes said to me as they approached. "what size tennis shoes is them?"

I looked down at the brand new Michael Johnson track Nikes that I had on and replied, "You don't want these size eights, joe. They came with blood on 'em."

"Is that right?" The dude said and sneered, "Whose blood?"

My answer came in the form of a two-piece combination that bust the dudes nose and mouth. He grabbed at his face as I leapt at his man and hit him with a four-piece combination of extra crispy punches that made him turn around and run. The whole day room was watching as I asked the dude whose face was dripping blood, "You still want these shoes? I told you they came with blood on 'em."

"Naw, I didn't want them." The dude said through bloody lips and teeth.

"Anybody else in here want these shoes?" I asked taking my T shirt off.

I could see all the lips that instantly twisted up, but nobody said a word, so I went back to my workout.

"Fuller!" Counselor Hinnent called out as he walked in the day room. "I see that you're back, huh?"

"Yeah, for a little while." I replied.

"What they got you for?"

"Some bodies. Same shit as last time."

"You wouldn't happen to be the reason that them two youngins over there need to go to the infirmary, would you?"

"Naw, Hinnent. I'm chilling. You know me."

"Yeah, you're right. I do know you. That's what I'm afraid of. But listen if one more muthafucka come through my office door fucked up, I'm blame you and I'ma lock your ass down until it's time for you to go to pop. You got me?"

"I got you." I replied and did my set of push-ups.

****

That evening at shower time, I walked into the shower room. I was dressed in boxers and my Oak Hill boots, tied up extra tight. Doing a mental check of all the showers and who was in them. The dude in the middle shower was my target. He was the man with the juice. He was light-skinned with curly hair, about my height, but a little thicker than me. It didn't matter. I walked straight up to him, stood about two feet in front of him and said, "I'm tryna get wet, joe."

"You got four other showers in here, homes. You might wanna try one of them." The dude replied.

Before I could react to the challenge, a short brown-skinned dude with cornrowed braids stepped out of the side shower and said, "Get in right here, Redds."

The little dude calling me by my nickname made me look at him closer. No recognition hit me. "I preciate that, joe, but I think I like the middle joint better. To the light-skinned, curly haired dude, I said, "You ain't gon let me get wet?"

"You what I said the first time." light-skinned replied.

"You're right." I walked out of the shower area and posted up on the wall. The short dude got out of the water, grabbed a towel, and dried off. He walked up to me and said,

"Slim, I'm hip to. I was at the Receiving Home with you when you fucked Gino up. And I was down Seven A with you. You are a cold blooded man and I respect that, but my man you tryna go at is too. Lil Joe ain't no sucker, slim you, me, and him…we're the same type of niggas. We ain't tryna beef with you slim, but you gotta ease up.

We recognize your gangsta, but you gotta calm down. I know how this shit go and you gotta challenge the nigga with the clout. But in this situation, you ain't gotta do that. He from the Southside, I'm from the Southside, and you from the Southside.

Them uptown niggas and Northeast niggas done got deep down here. We gotta stick together. On my honor, as a man, I'm being straight up with you. My man ain't tryna see you unless you press the issue. I told him who you are and how you get down, but he's a real nigga, too.

He ain't backing down from no challenge. So, now I'm asking you to back down. Although we just really met, officially, do that for me and one day I'ma return the favor."

I looked at the dude in the middle shower and then at the little brown-skinned dude. What he said sounded sincere and in so many words, he was letting me know that it was them against me if I didn't back down. I thought about what he said about the Uptown dudes getting deep and the Northeast dudes stretching. Then I decided that I was better off with friends and not too many enemies. It was time for me to get off my 'me against the world' shit. "A'ight, then, joe. I feel that." I walked back to the dude in the middle shower. "What's your name, joe?"

"Joe." He replied. "Joe Ebron."

I reached out and offered my hand to him. He shook it. "Dirty Redds, joe. I'ma chop it up with you after my shower."

"A'ight."

I slid in the shower that the little dude vacated and took my shower.

****

In the dayroom, I talked to Joe and the lil' dude. "Where you from Joe?"

"18th Street down by Anacostia, but I be down by Mario's."

"And you." I asked the short dude.

"I'm from Southwest." He replied.

"My antennas went up instantly. I was ready to fight some more.

The short dude read my body language. "Not that Southwest, slim. I know you beefing with them niggas. I'm from the other side of Southwest by Eastover. I be on Elmira, Forrester, and Galveston Streets. That's my hood."

We chopped it up until it was time to lock in our cells. As we were about to separate, I stopped the short dude.

"What's up, slim?" he asked.

"We been kicking it all this time and I still don't know your name."

"Oh, my bad, moe. It's Mousey, Lil Mousey."

****

"Fuller! Luther Fuller!"

"Yeah, damn. What's up?" I asked the counselor.

"Go to the chow hall. You gotta visit." He replied.

I went to my cell and took a quick bird bath, then got dressed in my fresh Oak Hill clothes. I walked from Seven B unit to the chow hall. On the weekends it doubled as the visiting room. When I walked into the room, I couldn't help but smile. My big homie Damien Lucas and Kemie stood up to embrace me. After we embraced, Damien said,

"I'ma slide over here to these vending machines and let you holla at Kemie." Then he left.

I looked Kemie up and down and liked what I saw. Kemie was a bad young chick and she knew it. Her jeans were tight, showing off her curves and her sweater did very little to hide the fact that her breasts were big. A pair of small Coach Loafers matched the Coach bag in her hand.

"Damn, you look good, boy. Your waves got me seasick." Kemie teased.

I ran my hand over my head. "It's good to see you, joe. No bullshit. I miss you like shit."

"Do you really? Cause I can't tell. You don't write me as much as I write you. You don't call that much. I can't tell you miss me."

"I be in this joint trying to stay alive for real. This shit is gladiator camp for real. I'm in here with all the niggas that I beef with in the streets. The only reason that these niggas ain't really brought me a move is because I got real street knives in here.

"Street knives? Naw, not you Sugar Ray Leonard. The last time I talked to you, you told me that nobody can see you with the hands. What changed?"

"The rules of the game changed. Plus, ain't nobody from Capers down here but Worm bitch ass and fat Sam. These niggas ain't tryna fight me, they know I'm a beast with my hands. They tryna jump a nigga now. So, I keep them street knives on me and I'ma bust their asses whenever they try it."

"Well, I'm not tryna talk about that. When are you coming home?"

"I don't know for sure. They still haven't indicted me."

"Why is it taking them so long to indict you, then?"

"I don't know. Maybe they still tryna get all their witnesses together. They gotta let me go in three months, anyway. So, I'm just chilling and waiting."

"That'll be nine months won't it? Then what?"

"Yeah. If they don't indict by then, I come home. If they do, then we go to trial after that."

"Well, I hope they don't indict so that you can come home."

"And why is that? Why you want me home?"

"Don't be dumb, boy. You know why I want you home. In four months, I'll be sixteen. And you know what happens then?"

I smiled at the thought of fucking Kemie in four months.

"Now, look at your pressed ass. Smiling all hard and shit. I knew that would make you start cheesing. With your geeking ass."

"I'm definitely geeking. As a matter of fact, are you scared of these people down here?"

"Why would I be scared of these people? I ain't locked

up. What can they do to me?"

"That's your word, huh?" I asked Kemie, baiting her right on in.

"Yeah, that's my word. Why? What are you up to?"

"I been in this joint for six months and all I see and semll is other niggas. I'm sick of that shit. It's driving me crazy. So, I need you to put your hand in your pants and rub it all over your pussy and let me smell it."

"What!" Kemie exclaimed. "You must be crazy, boy. I ain't…"

"You scared, joe. Either that or that pussy stink."

"Boy, you retarded. My pussy don't never stink and I'm not scared."

"Then do what I just told you to do, I need that."

Kemie looked around the sitting room first. Then her hand went under the table. I heard her jeans unzipping. I saw her still looking around as she did what I asked. Finally, she zipped back up and put her hand on the table. "How you gon' smell it?"

"Just give me your hand. Ain't nobody trippin' off us holding hands."

I moved around the table closer to Kemie, took her hand and smelled her fingers. Instantly, I frowned my face up.

"What? How it smell?" Kemie asked.

"Smell like piss." I said.

"Boy, stop. My pussy don't smell…let me smell it." Kemie smelled her fingers.

I bust out laughing. "Naw, I'm just playing. It smells good."

"I already know it do. Smells like soap and fruits of nature."

Grabbing her hand, I took it and sniffed it long and hard. "Yeah. I smell that. I can't even smell the pussy smell."

"Ain't no pussy smell. That's for them dirty bitches."

"Here come Damien. I love you, baby. Don't never for that. You hear me?"

Damien walked up and sat at the table.

"Let me holla at Dee right quick, Kemie."

Once Kemie left the table, I leaned over to Damien and asked, "Did you bring me something?"

"You know I did, youngin. It's in the skittles bag and the rest is in the Fritos bag. I'ma leave a few dollars with my Skip at the entrance. He gon' get it to you."

"Thanks, joe. You always come through for me. I don't know where I'd be without you. No bullshit."

"You'd be a'ight, but hey, I love you youngin. You like the little brother I never had. Check this out, though. I found out who the rat was. Some nigga named Troy…"

"Richardson. I know exactly who he is."

"Well, you ain't gotta worry about him. Never again. You feel me?"

"You knocked him off?" I silently mouth to Damien.

He nodded. "That's how you do them rats. Speaking of which, you got one right down here with you, close to you.

"Worm?" I asked.

Damien nodded again. "I ain't sure, but his name came up in your investigation."

"He wasn't even outside with us that night or with us on the moves."

"Like I said, his name came up. Just watch him and don't tell him nothing about your case. That nigga Omar still made because you shot him. I had to step to him and tell him to stop running his mouth before I crush him and Devan."

"What's up with slim? He out the wheel chair?"

"Yeah. And he's really your biggest fan, but Omar gon make me smoke both of their asses. Because if I smoke O, I ain't letting Devan stick around to seek revenge. That's out. So, hopefully Omar caught my drift when I hollered at him."

"Y' all heard from Bean over the jail?"

"Yeah. He good. I be sending him shit over there. I told him about the rat Troy. He knows that y' all should be coming home soon."

"That's what's up, slim, I really appreciate you. I love you, joe."

"I already know. You go ahead and finish hollering at Kemie. I'm ready to bounce. I got shit to do, youngin."

I grabbed the Fritos, skittles, and other snacks. "I'ma call you this week."

"Do that. I'm out."

I talked to Kemie for about twenty more minutes and then her and Damien left. I walked back to my unit thinking about Kemie. Then about Esha and Mildred. I thought about the way Kemie pussy smelled. I thought about fucking her in a few months. I thought about eating her. I went to my cell and closed the door. I covered up the glass on the door so nobody would peep in. I kept the light out as I thought the times that I fucked Esha and Mildred. I unzipped my jeans and pulled out my dick. And for the first time in my entire life I, I masturbated.

****

"Hey, Strong, come here for a minute, joe."

"What's up, Dirty Redds.?"

I pulled out a quarter bag of the raw dope that Damien left me. All the young dudes around me was on dope and I had what they needed. "You tryna hit this. Who quarter right here?" I flashed the bag on Strong.

"Hell, yeah, moe, what's up? What you need?"

"You know my homie Worm that live in 9 A?"

"Yeah, I know him. What's up?"

I handed Strong the small baggie of dope. "I need you to go and fuck him up. Take somebody with you. Don't even tell him why fucking him up. Just do it. Can you handle that?"

"Man, Dirty Redds, I'm on his ass first thing in the morning. Believe it."

"A'ight, homie. Good looking. Let your men know I got that raw, too."

****

Three months later it was like dejavu. The government dismissed the charges against me and Bean on the bodies. When we walked outside Damien was out there in his silver Convertible Mercedes Benz S600. He took me and Bean to Lifestyles and bought us a rack of shit, then dropped us off around the way. Bay One threw us a welcome party and everybody was there. While everybody was getting high and or drunk, or dancing, or whatever. Esha snuck upstairs and sucked my dick real good. Twice I was glad to be home.

****

"Bet that money in your hand to this money, my dog'll eat that shit up." Doug Quender from 18th and D challenged me as I walked Charmin.

"Doug, you don't wanna do that." I told Doug. "My bitch certified."

"Fuck all that. I got two grand right there to whatever you got in your pocket that Sheba will crush that joint."

"Naw, dawg. I'm good." I said and kept walking.

Doug pulled his Infiniti over and parked. "C'mon Dirty

Redds. One fight, slim. One break. Winner take all."

"You pick that spot. It don't matter to me."

We took the Pitbulls behind 601 on the Lawndry Court. Just him and me and the pits. I stood across from him and took the leash and collar off of Charmin. He did the same to his jet black pitbull. We held both dogs as they barked and jumped in anticipation of getting at the other.

"You ready?" Doug asked me.

"When you're ready. Make the call."

"Break!" Doug called out. "Get her Sheba!"

The two pitbulls attacked one another with a frenzy. They wrestled and nipped trying to gain position. Doug's pit was in good shape and looked to be stronger then my pit. The next thing I know, Charmin was flipped and Sheba was locked onto her underside. Charmin yelped in pain.

"Break!" Doug called out and smacked his pits ass. She let Charmin go. I was mad as shit, that I lost. "One more break, dawg." I told Doug. I pulled a knot of money out of my pocket. "One more break."

"Let's do it. Get your dog ready."

I grabbed Charmin and tried to put her in front of Sheba. But to my surprise, Charmin turned on and faced me.

"Your dog said, naw, slim. Gimme my money." Doug said laughing.

I tossed Doug the money and whipped out my brand new Glock .40. It was a beautiful 10 shot joint that I'd gotten from Damien.

"Hold on, slim. Take it easy, it ain't that serious. Here you can have your money back. You ain't gotta shoot me."

"Ain't nobody gon shoot your scared ass." I said and fired two bullets into Charmin's head. "I should've been killed her ass. She take after her father. He was a bitch."

Walking back down the streets, I ran into Tee. Just seeing

him looking all dusty and shit, made me irritable.

"Dirty Redds, let me hold something until a better day." Tee said.

"Nigga, if I do, it'll rain shit cakes on Christmas."

"Damn, lil homie, don't be so mean. I'm get back right in a minute."

Paying Tee no mind, I bent the corner and headed towards Kemie's house. I knocked on her door and waited. When she answered the door, I pulled her into my arms.

"What's wrong, Redds?" Kemie asked.

"I just killed my dog." I replied and wept like a baby.

****

"How you doing, Ms. Brenda? Where Kemie at?"

"She's in the house, Redds. Come on in."

Kemie rushed down the stairs and leapt into my arms. She hugged me tight. "Happy Birthday, baby."

"Thank you. So, what do you have planned for today?" Kemie asked me.

"It's your birthday, you call it. I'll call things later." I winked.

Kemie punched me in the shoulder. "Yeah, I bet you will, nasty ass self."

"Straight up though, what you wanna do? I got the Benz from Damien, so we can go wherever you want to go. It's up to you."

"You know that I am a simple girl. I don't need much. A movie and a meal. It don't matter as long as we're together. That's all that matters to me."

"I got the perfect place for the meal. What movie are you tryna see?" I asked.

"I wanna see that new Dave Chappelle movie. Half

Baked, I think it is. Everybody says that it's funny as shit."

"I heard about that joint, Kemie. It's funny, but you gotta be high to get it. I mean, to really get it."

"You ain't said nothing but a word. Tonight is the night that I become a woman. So, I might as well smoke a little weed. Besides, I might need to be high for later. They say weed and drink dulls the pain. You got some weed?"

I nodded my head. "I got both weed and drink at my house."

"Well, let's go to your first, then to the movies. After that we eat and then you get desert."

"That sounds like a plan to me. Let's go."

****

Me and Kemie saw Half Baked high as hell and we laughed hysterically through the whole movie. After leaving the Mulitplex Movie Theater in Virginia, we went to the BET soundstage restaurant for food. Every table had a small T.V. screen in the booth. So we watched BET on TV as we ate food from their buffet.

"This fried fish is good as hell." Kemie remarked.

"I'm hip. All this shit taste good to me. I ain't never had no catfish before but it's gooder than a muthafucka. But it ain't fuckin' with this fried cabbage and mac & cheese."

After the waiter cleared the table I gave Kemie three square boxes. Her eyes got as big as saucers.

"Redds…what's this?"

"It's your birthday presents, that's what. Open 'em."

The smile on Kemie's face was priceless. She opened the first box and pulled at the Tiffany toggle bracelet. I helped her put it on her wrist. Then she opened the next box and pulled out the matching ankle bracelet.

"Put your foot in my lap and let me put it on you." I told her.

Kemie lifted her leg and hiked up her jeans. I pulled off the Gucci shoes she had on her left foot and stared at her pretty feet. Her toenails were painted red with the tiny initials LF on each big toe. "You weren't supposed to see that until tonight. I got your initials put on my toes because they belong to you. I belong to you."

I put the bracelet around her ankle. "Open the last box."

In the last box was a gold link chain and a solid gold heart pendant.

"Look at the back of the heart."

Kemie flipped the heart over. It read... 'My heart L.F.'

"Baby it's beautiful." Kemie said as tears came to her eyes. "I remember when I was seven years old. The day I went looking for you because you hadn't been to school. When I found you in your old house after your mother's death, I knew then, that we would be together. I know then that I would give myself to you and only you. I'm ready to go home. I'm ready to be yours in every way. Let's go."

****

My seduction of Kemie was slow and meticulous. She lay beneath me completely nude and trembling. I wanted her to relax, so I kissed her mouth for what seemed like an eternity. Then I went around to her neck and kissed and licked her there. I moved down to each breast and paid attention to each nipple. Kemie's moans became more pronounced, more vocal.

Her body responded to my seductive touches. I kissed her navel and took a finger to spin circle around her clit. My finger became soaking wet as I forced about an inch into

Kemie's tight pussy. Then I replaced my finger with my tongue. That drove Kemie crazy.

Her body spasmed as if she'd been hit with a taser. Her hands gripped my head and tried to pull me off, but I wasn't going away. I was there to stay, so I locked my mouth onto Kemie's pussy and put my tongue as far as it would go inside her. I put it on her clit and licked and sucked her there. Kemie made a fist and punched my head lightly.

"St-o-o-p-p! I...I...can...t...take...ta...ke...that! R-e-e-d-ds...ple-e-e-a-a-s-e, st-o-o-p! It...f-e-e-e-l...too...go-o-o-oo-od!"

I gripped Kemie's legs firm under her and made her take the pleasure of my tongue. I forced it into her. Her juices coated my face and tasted good in my mouth. Kemie, tasted sweet as if she'd been eating nothing, but pineapples all day. My dick was rock hard the entire time and begging for some attention. It was time to give him what he wanted. I slithered back up Kemie's body. She tensed in anticipation of what she knew was about to happen.

"Relax." I told her. "I'ma go slow and I'ma be gentle."

"Okay. Go ahead."

"Open your legs some more. Don't be scared. Open 'em."

I eased that dick into Kemie a little at a time. I felt the tightening loosen as I pushed passed the outer barrier. Kemie gripped my back and dug her nails in me as I pushed myself deeper into her.

"Here, take the pillow and bite on it. We almost there. It's already in you."

Kemie turned her face to the side and used one hand to hold the pillow as she bit down on it. The other hand stayed on my back, fingernails still dug into my skin. I journeyed on until I was all the way inside Kemie. She whimpered and wiggled and tried to back up, but again I refused that request.

Her legs tried to close around me and I denied that request, too. Using my arms, I locked her knees in the crooks of my arms and dug deeper. It felt so good and tight and wet that I struggled to not bust a nut. The only thing that helped me was the weed. The weed acted as a deterent for me coming early. After a while Kemie calmed down and got into it. That made the situation better. She was able to get rid of the pillow and take the dick without it. We kissed. She bit my lips and wrapped her arms around me tightly. She squeezed me so hard that I almost told her to ease up. But I didn't. I felt myself about to cum. My breathing became labored.

"Don't cum in me, Redds." Kemie moaned.

"I'm not." I replied and pulled my dick out of her.

It erupted all over her pubic hairs, which were trimmed and pretty. I was tired as hell from the long day, the weed, and the sex, so I just laid down on Kemie.

"Redds, let me go and clean myself up."

"For what? We gon' do it again in a minute."

"That's fine, but I still need to clean up."

I lifted up off of Kemie and turned over. I laid on the bed and watched Kemie's phat ass jiggle as she pulled on a robe and went to the bathroom. I could hear the shower water running. I used the sheet on her bed to wipe my dick off. I couldn't resist the urge. I was ghetto. I laid there and thought about what had just happened and smiled.

I had finally gotten Kemie's goodies. I had to wait eight years to get 'em, but it was worth it to me. To me, everything about our love was complete. It was full circle. One day, we'd have children and really be a family. If I could just manage to live that long to accomplish it. About twenty minutes later, Kemie came out of the bathroom.

As she dropped the robe and stood nude at the foot of the bed, something about her looked different. As if she'd had a metamorphosis since losing her virginity. She crawled up the bed and laid on me.

"I'm ready for round two." She whispered.

I positioned Kemie on top of me and put the dick back in her. I taught her how to ride me and girlfriend took it from there. After a few rounds, I realized that Kemie was a natural.

****

For the next couple months, I spent less time in the streets and more time with Kemie at her house. Her mother, Brenda was still getting high and the money that I gave her daily fed her addiction. So she was never home. Kemie and I had the house to ourselves and acted like a real married couple. When she got out of school, she came straight home and cooked. We fucked like newlyweds and enjoyed each other's company. My life at that point had calmed down.

The beefs with the Gardens and 15th Street was damn near non-existent and the city was getting niggas paid. Like the eighties. I copped coke from Damien, cooked it and fronted it out to all my young homies. My guns were getting cold and life was good. Then three months later in the summer of 1999, all of that changed. The streets wouldn't let me chill…

I was in the house with Kemie when my beeper went off incessantly. Everybody from the hood beeped me and put 911 in my beeper. I called Bay One back first. In my mind I thought that something had happened with Marquette, but I wasn't sure.

"Dirty Redds," Bay One said and then paused, "I'm…sorry, boo…but…" My inpatience made me explode. "Boy, what the fuck is up? You're sorry about what? Did something happen to Quette? Somebody did something to my uncle?"

"Naw, boo. It's not your uncle. It's Damien. Somebody killed Damien."

I dropped the phone and fell to my knees. My emotions hit me instantly and I felt a pain deep inside me. That I hadn't felt since my mother was killed. My cries got louder.

"Dirty Redds? Dirty Redds!" Bay One screamed into the phone. But I couldn't answer. Kemie rushed down the steps and grabbed me.

"Baby... what happened?" Kemie screamed as she held me. "Redds, what's wrong? Why are you crying? Redds!"

"What's going on down here?" Brenda Bryant asked from the stairs.

"I don't know." Kemie told her. "I heard Redds crying and came in here."

"What is he crying for?"

"Ma, I said I don't know. Get the phone and see who's on it."

Brenda Bryant picked up the phone off the floor. "Hello? Who is...Bay One? What? Oh...My...God!"

"Ma...what is it? What happened?"

"Somebody killed Damien Lucas."

"Shit! Baby...I'm sorry!"

I kneeled on that floor and saw my whole life flash before me. I saw all the intimate moments that me and Damien shared. All the things he'd taught me. I saw everything that he'd given me. I remembered the Oak Hill visits. The stuff he smuggled me and the counselors he paid off so that I would be comfortable while locked up.

All I could see in my head was his face. The dark skin, the low tapered haircut with spinning waves, his white teeth perfect, except for a chip on his front tooth. I could hear his voice. And he was reminding me that if anybody crossed me, to kill them. By killing Damien, somebody had definitely killed a part of me. So, it was time to kill again.

Whoever, wherever. No matter how many. Somebody was about to die. I picked myself up off the floor and wiped my eyes, now embarrassed at my moment of weakness. I had to pry myself from Kemie's arms.

"Redds, what are you about to do?" Kemie asked.

Ignoring her, I gathered my keys, beeper, and stuff that was on the table and pocketed everything. Then I ran upstairs and got my twin Glock fourties from under Kemie's bed. I came down the stairs.

Kemie saw the guns and threw herself on me. "No-o-o...Redds! Please! Please don't do go! Please...Noooo!"

"Get off me!" I said throwing Kemie off me.

"Ma! Please! Get him! Tell him I need him! Tell him not to go!"

"I can't, Kemie!" Brenda Bryant surrendered. "Let him go!"

"N-O-O-O-O-O-O! N-OO-O-O!"

I left Kemie's house oblivious to her cries that followed me down the block. I ran all the way to Bay One's house. When I walked in, everybody was packed in the small living room. Everybody's eyes were glued to the two handguns in my hands. "Who did it? Who did it?"

Bay One spoke up. "Dirty Redds, nobody knows yet. He was..."

"How the fuck can nobody know shit?" I exploded.

"Baby boy, please calm down and put them guns away." Bay One pleaded.

I lifted my shirt and put both Glocks in the waist of my jeans. I leaned on the wall away from everybody else and asked, "What happened?"

Marquette spoke next. "His grandmother, Ms. Porter,

called me. She was hysterical. She said that the police con-
tacted her and told her that they found two bodies in the
woods behind Stanton Hill apartments. A man and a woman.
They said they found the bodies two days ago, but just identified them. Damien was identified by his fingerprints in the
system. Ms. Porter's number was in their system. She said
the cops told her that Damien was bound, gagged, and shot
in the head. Him and the woman were found the same way
and then killed the same way.

"'I swear to God...I swear to God...I'ma kill everybody..."

"Dirty Redds? Let me holla at you outside, slim."

I looked up and saw Bean motioning for me to follow
him out the door. When we were on the front porch alone,
Bean said, "Do you notice who ain't here?"

I shook my head. "Naw, joe. Who you talking 'bout?"

"Go and look and see who you don't see."

I walked back into Bay One's house and did a visual
search of the entire room. Everybody that I could think was
present. Bowlegged Dion and Wayne Wayne had both gotten
locked up recently on murder beefs. Then it dawned on me
who was missing. I went back to the porch. "Creeko and Tee."

Bean nodded. "The main two niggas that be with Damien
the most outside of Marquette. And check this out, while you
been bunned with wifey, Damien came through looking for
Creeko a few weeks ago, mad as shit. He told me that Creeko
and Tee both owed him some money and ain't pay it. I think
the money Tee owed was some short shit, but Creeko owed
the most.

He told me that he was gonna beat both of their asses
when he caught them. Now this happens. And neither one of
them niggas ain't nowhere to be found. Damien been dead
two days, your uncle just said, but my gut tells me that it was

one of them niggas who did it or had something to do with it. You know Damien just as well as me.

He don't never slip. Can't just anybody get up on him like that. Plus, how many niggas outside of our circle know Damien had that spot on Stanton Hill? Then to get him like that to where he was tied up and all that bamma ass shit… that was the work of a muthafucka he trusted."

I thought about everything Bean said. It all had that ring of truth to it. I thought about the last time I'd been to the Stanton Hill apartment and the darkskinned female that answered the door each time. We had never exchanged a word, nor had I ever been told her name. "I feel you, joe. I'ma make some noise and get to the bottom of it and when I do, everybody involved with my man's death is going to die."

****

"Oh-Creeko…Oooh…Creeko…you   fucking…the shit…outta…me!"

"Whose pussy is this? Whose is it?"

"It's yours! It's your pussy! Creeko!"

"Who else you been fucking?"

"Nobody! Nobody, but you!"

The bedspring crooked with every thrust. For a minute or so, I thought the bed was gonna break and crush me, but it held. The boxspring that the mattress laid on was strong and sturdy. Slowly, quietly, I slid from underneath the bed. Once out from under it, I pulled my Glock .40 out of my waist. Beside the bed was a small stack of potatoes.

In his haste to get some pussy, Creeko never saw the potatoes sitting by the bed. Or if he did, he never said anything to his companion or tied to move them. I took one of the potatoes and forced the barrel of my 40 into it. The noise that

I made was drowned out by the creaking bedspring. Creeko lived on Jay Street in Capital Hill, not too far from the hood. I'd broken into his house earlier and waited for him to come. Hours later he did.

"Oooh, Creeko! Creeko, fuck me! Creeko!"

"You like this dick, don't you?"

"I love it, Creeko! I love it!"

I rolled over onto my stomach and stood up slowly. The woman that Creeko was fucking saw me first.

"Aye!" She screamed and pushed Creeko off her. "Creeko, look!"

Creeko turned in my direction and moved off of the woman. She gripped the covers in her hand, keeping them pulled up past her breasts. The room was semi dark, but I could still see that the woman with Creeko was a beauty. She was one that I'd never seen before, but it didn't surprise me, Creeko was known for having all bad bitches on his team. "Dirty Redds…what the fuck…slim? Fuck you doing in my house?"

"You know why I'm here big homie." I told him.

"I didn't have nothing to do with Damien getting robbed and killed, slim. I swear that on my father's grave. It wasn't me. Damien was my man. You know that."

"And this how you mourn his death, joe."

"What do you want me to do? I've cried already."

"I think you were with it, Creeko. So go ahead and say your prayers."

"Slim, go ahead with that bullshit. You gon' kill me over some shit that Theodore put together. I didn't have nothing to do with that shit. Swear to God, I didn't."

"Theodore? So, Tee is responsible for Damien's death?"

"He told me that Damien threatened him about 1000 dollars that he owed Damien. He was fucked about it. Said that all of us come up from the dirt and now that Damien was getting a rack of money, he was acting funny. He said that Damien had changed and all that."

"Did he tell what he wanted to do to Damien? Rob him or whatever?"

"He mentioned it, but I didn't pay him no mind. You know Tee be snorting that shit, so I just pressed it off as a dope rant. I never thought that he'd really do that shit."

"You never thought he'd really do it, huh? But you knew about it though, right?"

"Slim, I just told you that, he mentioned it, but I paid him no mind."

"What did he mention? I need to know what he said. Word for word. Was he going to rob Damien or rob him and kill him? Or did he mention somebody else doing it?"

"I don't remember him mentioning no names, but he knew he couldn't do that shit by himself. He knew how Damien operated. He'd have to take somebody with him."

"Any idea who that somebody might be?"

"Probably his cousin Rico from Frederick Place and Stanton Terrace."

"I don't know if I believe you or not, big homie, but you are just as guilty as Tee for what happened to Damien, even if you wasn't with it."

"How the fuck am I guilty? I wasn't with that shit."

"Did you tell anybody about what Tee said to you?"

"Naw, but..."

"Did you holla at Damien and give him a heads up?"

"I thought Tee was just venting because he been fucked up for so long and now he getting high. I never thought he'd go through with it."

"You never thought...you didn't think...excuse, joe. Did you put Damien on point about what Tee told you? Yes or

No?"

Defeat registered in Creeko's eyes. "Naw, slim. I didn't."

"And that's why I gotta kill you, slim. For Damien."

"Don't do it…don't do…"

Phop! Phop!

I shot Creeko in the face. The back of his head exploded and blood and brains coated the pillow and sheets under him. The female got one long scream off before I shot her. I moved closer to the bed and fired several more shots into both of their bodies. Then I spotted the potatoes by the bed. I stuffed them all in my pocket. There was one that couldn't fit so I did the next best thing, I ate it.

****

"Joe, I always wondered whether I'd feel different after killing a bitch."

"Do you feel different?" Bean asked.

"Naw, not at all. Killing bitches ain't no different than killing niggas. It feels the same."

"How did she look? The bitch that was with Creeko?"

"She was a bad muthafucka, joe. The light was out, but the moonlight illuminated the room enough for her to see me and for me to see her. She had one of them short haircuts like that old Toni Braxton cut. She was brown-skinned she was pretty as shit. He was fucking her when I rolled from under the bed. I know one thing, she talked that talk while he had that dick in her."

Bean laughed. "I wonder did anybody find them yet?"

"If so, we ain't heard nothing about it. Fuck that nigga, joe. He had it coming. He admitted that Tee told him that he was gon' pull that shit and he ain't tell nobody."

"Ain't nobody seen Tee yet, huh?"

"Naw, you seen him?"

"Fuck you mean, have I seen him. If I'd have seen him, he'd been still stuck to the pavement somewhere. You think you the only one that loved Damien? Nigga, I'ma bake his ass if I catch him. Do some real wicked shit to him and then kill him. I might fuck that nigga."

It was my turn to laugh. "Yeah, whatever. You wouldn't fuck that nigga, joe."

"You shittin' me! I'd burn that nigga ass up, then skeet in him to make 'em feel real fucked up. Like he a cold blooded bitch. Then I'd kill him and set his ass on fire to hide that I went in his ass."

"You lunchin' like shit, then. I wouldn't go that far. There go the spot right there. Park in front of that joint." I told Bean.

"Off Da Hook Tattoos, huh? You dead serious about getting that tattoo, huh?"

"Yeah, joe. I gotta get this joint. C'mon."

We walked up the stairs and entered the tattoo parlor. There was a slim, brown-skinned dude at the front desk. He had tattoos everywhere.

"What's up, joe. I'm tryna get a tattoo."

"Who, both of y'all?" the dude asked.

"Naw, just me." I replied.

"What are you tryna get, moe? And where are you getting it?"

I lifted my shirt and forgot that I had both of my Glock.40's in my waist. Both of the butts could be visibly seen. The dudes eyes dropped to my weapons. "My bad, joe, I forgot I had these with me. But anyway, I'm tryna get that tat right here across my chest, big as shit. Two sentences."

"And what's that? The two sentences?"

"God, please protect me from my friends. I can handle my enemies."

"A'ight. I'm ready right now. My name's Paul. Let's do it."

Two days later, Me, Bean, and Pee Wee were down the rec shooting pool and smoking trees. As soon as we walked out, we ran into Esha, Reesie, Marnie, Dawn, Lil Kesha, Yoni, Miesha, and Kemie. I walked up on Kemie and grabbed her. I held her around the waist and kissed her deeply.

"Hey, baby." Kemie said after our kiss.

"What's up with you?" I responded back.

"Shit. Just came from the carryout."

"Where the food at?"

"I ate it. You know I don't be playing with that beef and broccoli. As soon as I got mine, I started fucking it up, right there in the carryout."

"Damn, you greedy as shit. Didn't even ask me if I wanted anything."

"I didn't know where you was at. I saw Tee going in your father's shop, so I thought you was in there, but you wasn't. I…"

"Hold up…wait. When did you see Tee go in the barber-shop?"

"About 10 minutes ago. Why?"

I ignored Kemie's last question. Anger washed over me and the beast inside me roared. "Aye, Bean, Tee is at the bar-bershop." I said and made a beeline for the barbershop. I never looked back but I knew that Bean was on my heels. It took me five minutes to reach the barbershop on 8th Street. I walked up and peeped into the plate glass window of the shop. There was Tee. Sitting in one of the chairs getting his haircut, smiling and joking with the dude was cutting his hair. A second glance revealed that he was seated in the chair right next to the one my father had a dude in cutting his hair.

"You can't hit him in there, slim. We'll wait until he comes out here." Bean commented. "His ass is done."

Seeing Tee sitting, there rapping and laughing made my blood boil. Suddenly, I couldn't wait. I headed for the door of the shop.

"Dirty Redds, where you going? What you…?"

"You know what I'm about to do." I hissed.

"You gon' do it in there in front of all them people?"

"Watch me."

I walked into the barbershop and focused directly on Tee. He spotted me and his smile turned upside down. Our eyes locked as I pulled both Glocks.

"Bitch nigga, you gotta answer for Damien." I pointed the gun at him.

"Dirty Redds, it wasn't me! It was Creeko!"

"Son, what the hell are you doing?" My father asked. "Put them guns up! Now!"

"Can't do it, Pops. Tee killed Damien. He gotta go."

Tee threw his hands up in a sign of surrender. "It wasn't me! It wasn't me!"

"Luther. Put them guns down, now, son! Put 'em down!"

Oblivious to everybody but Tee, I walked up closer to him. "For Damien."

I fired both guns. Tee's body jumped with every entrance of lead. He tried to stand as I hit his ass. But the force of my bullets made him stick to the barber chair. I hit Tee so many times in the face that it was unrecognizable. "For Damien." I muttered again before I was grabbed from behind and slammed to the ground.

In minutes, the barbershop was filled with cops. As I was lead out of the in cuffs. I looked across the street and looked Bean leaning on the wall. Our eyes locked and then nodded his head. I nodded back.

****

At the homicide building, all of my clothes were taken and I was given a white paper suit to wear. Detectives tried to interview me but I refused it. While I was being lead outside to a transport vehicle that was taking me to the Central Cell Block, I saw a detective that worked on my other case, a few years ago.

"Finally got your bad ass, huh? Dirty Redds. Fucked up this time and killed a dude in a public place in front of a lot of witnesses. Got your ass now."

"Fuck you." I told him.

"Naw, not me. But that's what them adults gon' do over the jail when you get there. Ain't no more Oak Hill for you, buddy. You're in the big leagues now. You're a big boy. Don't drop that soap when you get over the jail. Asshole."

At Central Cell Block, I was processed and officially charged with first degree murder while armed. Early the next morning, I was taken to court, where judge ordered me held without bond and issued a title 16.

When I asked the lawyer the courts appointed me, what that was, he said, "You've been charged as an adult. You go to DC Jail's juvenile block and wait for trial. If you lose in trial, you stay there until you're eighteen and then you go to Lorton. I'll be over to the jail in a few weeks to see you. Take Care."

As the court bus rambled through the streets of D.C. I kept my face plastered to the window. I looked at the streets, the people moving around on them as if seeing it for the first time. All the while, thinking about where I was going. And where I'd been, Oak Hill. I thought about all the stories I'd heard about D.C. jails in famous juvenile block. It was my destiny to walk its tier. It would be a new obstacle for me. A new right of passage. New tests that I would have to pass as I continue to make my bones. Minutes after I got on the court bus, a song came on the radio that was playing in the bedroom the night I broke Kemie in. It made me think of her and how hurt she would be with my absence. Murder in the District was punishable by up to 40 years. I knew that there wouldn't be no more nine month bids and then I go home. I killed Tee in front of a whole shop full of people and there was no Damien Lucas and Creeko to bial me out of this one.

"You're in the big leagues now...ain't no more Oak Hill..."

The court bus pulled into the gates behind the D.C. Jail. I looked at the red brick façade of the jail and smiled. Another chapter of my life was about to start. Behind those walls were enemies and friends. I smiled again. "Let the games begin."

****

This is your DC number, Fuller. Remember it because it's gonna stick with you the rest of your life. 290-534. You got it? Okay. Strip. Let me see your hands, turn 'em over, lift up your arms, stick out your tongue, turn around and spread your cheeks, cough and squat, now for your feet...okay, get a bed roll from in the back and go to take a shower. Coco, hit him with the de-lice spray when he comes out the shower...next man..."

****

"'Northside!" The CO stated to the CO in the booth that controlled the doors that led to the North and Southsides. The hallway was spacious and music played on speakers that couldn't be seen. There were two of us juveniles headed to the juvenile block. Me and another tall dude who told me his name was Mecca Lee Bay. "North One, y' all got two coming."

A fat, older CO stepped up to the grill and grabbed two cards from the CO who escorted us.

"Luther Fuller and Mecca Lee Bay, let's see. Fuller, you going to the top left and Lee Bay, you're on the top right."

Inside the block was pure pandemonium. I walked past the police bubble and turned left. I walked up the stairs. The big steal and fiberglass door slid open. I walked on the tier straight to cell 30. Once I stepped in the cell and put my bed roll down the door closed.

"Aye, main man in 30 cell, where you from?" someone called out.

Kill my mother, moe, that look like this nigga I'm beefing with." Another dude said. "Pass me my banger."

The next thing I heard was the sound of someone sharpening something. From the stories I'd heard, I know it was a knife. "Shit." I muttered to myself and looked around the cell for something that I could make a weapon out of. There was nothing there.

"Aye, main man, this is the Uptown side over here. If you ain't from Northwest or Northeast, you need to call the police and tell them to move you."

I ignored the dude there was no way that I was calling the CO. It wasn't going to happen. I was gonna die at 16 years old on the dirty ass ceramic tile on the tier outside my cell. I'd heard all about the juvenile block, so I already knew that there were 4 tiers in the block, two upstairs, and two downstairs, called the top and bottom. I know that the bottom tiers housed adults on both sides. One was for special handling, which was dudes with high profile cases that couldn't be housed with anybody else in their case. And the other side was PC, protective custody. The top two tiers were for juveniles and the two sides, right and left were always beefing for no reason other than it wasn't nothing else to do.

"We gon' kill you in the morning, dawg." Somebody called out.

"You better check off the tier or die." Another said.

"I want his shoes. Y' all can have his life."

"If y' all hold him down, I'ma fuck him." one dude threatened.

"Yeah, me too."

"We gon' see about that." I muttered and made up the bed. If tomorrow was gonna be my last day living, I at least wanted to sleep good and be prepared to fight until I died. I smiled to myself and said, "These niggas got me fucked up."

I was up early the next morning prepared for whatever. I took the course, wool blanket and wrapped it around my upper body. I put the hygiene shit that the jail gave me in a pillow case and tied it up. It would have to make a good hammer, I tied my timberland boots up tight and waited for the door to open. A few minutes later, it opened and is stepped out the cell. The whole tier cracked up laughing. I looked at all the faces that came out of the cells. Almost everybody present, I knew. They were friends of mine from everywhere. I laughed too.

"Scared ass nigga got all that wild shit on." Joe Green said.

"Dirty Redds was ready to die." Lil' Mike from 1430 L Street said.

I dropped my makeshift hammer and leaned on the wall, relieved. Dudes moved in to hug me or shake my hand. On the tier with me was Lil' Mousey, Joe Ebron, Lil Marvin from Wellington Park, Black Pug, Lil' Face, Andre Bruno,

Michael "Pretty Bee" Winson, Lil Fat from 18th and D, Ronald Benn from Ridge Road, Ronnie T from Hillside, Big Syke from 1st and O, and Kee Kee Star from the Valley. Mousey stepped up and embraced me tight. Then he made a few more introductions.

"D-Roc, this is my man Dirty Redds. Redds that's D-Roc and That's his codefendant fella. They good men from sim-ple...I mean Alabama Avenue. This is J.T. from Park Chester and this is my man B.F. from Barry Farms. The rest of these niggas ain't nobody. We knew you was coming. I got a rack of shit in the cell for you."

"How long you been over here?" I asked.

"About four months. I'm fighting a double joint." Mousey replied.

"You by yourself?"

"Naw, me and my codefendant, Keith. He's on the other tier over there. I don't know why he's over there, but that's where he's at."

"Was he down the Hill with us?"

"Naw. This is his first bid. Who you kill this time?"

"One of my homies that had it coming. I'm stuck on this one, though, joe."

"I feel you. This one might be me, too. Depends on my scared ass codefendant."

"What's his name again?"

"Keith. Keith Barnett."

****

"Get ready, Fuller, you gotta social visit." The CO called out from the bubble. I wondered who my visitor could be. But knowing Kemie like I do, it wouldn't surprise me if she had convinced her mother or somebody in her family to bring her to DC Jail.

I pulled my crispy new sky blue jumpsuit from under the bed. Looking in the mirror I didn't see any difference in myself. I looked the same. And that was because nobody could read what was going on inside of me. Nobody knew the boiling pot of water that was in me. I continued to hide my real feelings from my men on the tier. Nobody would understand my pain. I went to the bubble and got cuffed to the belly down. Juveniles couldn't walk through the adult facility without restraints. And all adult traffic stopped when we moved through the jail. In the visiting hall, I learned that there were three cages, small individual cages, set aside for us. I was lead to a cage and out of nowhere a face appeared. It was a face that I never expected to see, ever.

"What's up, Pops?" I said as soon as I picked up the receiver.

"How you doing, son?" Luther Fuller, Sr. replied.

"I'm good Pops. What brought you here today?"

"I thought it was time that you and I talked."

"It took for me to kill a dude in front of you to get you finally notice me?"

"I deserve that, son. I really do. This ain't easy for me now. Don't make it harder for me."

"I dig that, but straight up, I feel like this conversation doesn't need to be had."

"If you want me to go, just say so and I'll leave."

"That's your decision to make, pop. I gotta sit here regardless until the people come back and get me."

"Listen son, and I don't use the term loosely because I've never been a father to you…"

"You took me in after my mother got killed. I respected that."

"But that short amount of time didn't make up for all the

time I've been away."

"Away? Your barbershop is right up the street from where I was raised. You weren't away. You just weren't there."

"You don't think I know that? You don't think I gotta live with that truth every day? I'ma say what I gotta say and you can either accept it or reject it. I just need to say it."

"I'm listening." I told my father. I couldn't help but to notice how much I looked like the man sitting on the side of the glass. His skin was the same as mine. The color of his hair and the texture of it was identical. His freckles had been passed on to me.

"I have other children, children that you've never met. I haven't been much of a father to any of them either. You have two sisters and three brothers. But you are the only Luther Fuller, besides me. When your mother and I were together, our relationship was volatile, it was pretty violent son.

We had to separate before one of us killed the other. Once she had you, she denied me all basic parental rights. When she started using drugs, she came to me demanding money. I gave it to her. Every time, then after a while I stopped. She refused to let me see you after that.

It became if you want to be in your son's life, you gotta give me money for drugs. I couldn't agree to that, so I stayed away. By the time she died and you came to me, I didn't know how to raise an eight-year old child. I was in between marriages and dealing with a lot of stuff. All of my kids' mothers were upset with me.

The only thing that kept me from going crazy was my shop. It's the only place where I felt any peace. Then a few weeks ago, you broke that peace. I had to watch my son, my flesh and blood, brutally murder a guy in one of my chairs. A kid that I've known his entire life. Theodore…"

"Needed a killing. I gave him what he needed."

"However you rationalize it in your head is on you, but son, I don't hate you for who you are, so don't hate me for who I am. A simple barber. That's who I am. Who I've always been. I've heard all the stories about you. Dirty Redds is what they call you. And everybody is afraid of the big bad wolf.

I know that you killed the men who did that to your mother. Those bastards deserved whatever you did t them. But what about all the other people you've killed? Did they deserve what you've done to them? I think about all the things that I've heard you've done and I question myself.

Where did you get all of the evil inside of you? The hate, the desire to kill? Where did it all come from? From me? From Margaret? Sometimes I blame myself for what you've become. Maybe if I'd have paid you more attention, your life would be different. Maybe if I'd had been a better father to you, maybe you wouldn't be here now.

There are days when I feel that this is all my fault. Is this my fault? Am I to blame for what you are? What you've become? And what can I do to change that direction of your life? Can we mend our relationship and become a better father and son? I need to know the answers to these questions, son."

I thought about everything my father said and decided to give him what I was feeling in the raw. Whether he was hurt by my words or not, he needed to hear them.

"I sat in a closet…well stood…and watched my mother get beat to death. Can you imagine how that felt? I was eight-years old. I lost a lot that that day. I lost a woman that I loved regardless of her imperfections.

I lost a mother who was supposed to guide my life down the right path. I lost my innocence. I lost any idea of a conscience. Living with you as a kid only made it worse. All you cared about was your barbershop. I was an eight-year old child that had to understand that and accept it. Cool.

I was raised by the streets and two people…my uncle and Damien Lucas. They taught me what my mother couldn't what you chose not to. And I'm cool with that. The evil inside me is my own. It didn't come from you or my mother. It was raised right inside of me. I'm the father of it.

The streets made me kill. I'm product of my environment. So, don't blame yourself for what I am. I'm good. I believe that my path was already designed for me before I was born. I'm just fulfilling my destiny. And nothing you could do at this point can change my path.

Can we mend our relationship? It was never broken to need mending. Why? Because it never existed. I'll be seventeen years old in a couple months. And in a year or so, I'll be a grown man in the eyes of the law. But I've been a man. My own man and I don't need you to be a father to a grown man. It's too late. Live your life. Reconnect with your other kids. I'm good, Pops. I don't need you."

"I wish that things could've been different between us, son. I really do."

"Yeah, me too."

Luther Fuller, Sr. hung up the receiver and walked away. He got his visiting paper from the bubble and then got a on the elevator. He never looked back.

****

I woke up the next morning to muffled screams. Then I heard grunts and what sounded like skin slapping together. My ears had to be deceiving me. My curiosity got the better of me and I ventured out of the cell. A crowd of dudes stood around the last cell on the tier. It had been empty yesterday. The muffled screams got louder the closer I got to the crowd. I saw Mousey and Black Pug standing on the side, so I approached them.

"What's going on, joe? Fuck is that noise?"

Mousey and Pug bust out laughing. Then Mousey said, "Dawg, you ain't gon' believe this shit. I still can't believe it."

"What? Fuck you talkin' bout?"

"Last night, they brought this nigga named Quincy on the tier. He from Conyers Park and he wicked as shit. He told on some good men back in like 95 or something. Big Syke and nem told the nigga that if he stayed on the tier that they were gonna fuck him in the morning. Gangsta rat nigga thought they were bullshittin'. I thought they were bullshittin'. Well, guess what? They weren't bullshittin'! Look at that shit."

Positioning myself between Mousey and Pug, I stood on my tiptoes and peered into the cell. And sure enough, a dude was in the bunk with his jumpsuit at his ankles. His boxers were at his ankles, too. As four different dudes held the dude down, Big Syke pounded himself into the dude. They had a sock stuffed in his mouth to muffle his screams. All I could do was shake my head. "Them some wild niggas, joe. No bullshit."

"Naw." Pug said. "What's wild is that they been fuckin' that nigga since the doors opened about forty minutes ago. Syke is like the third nigga that been in his ass."

"Man, fuck that nigga, joe. He's a rat and now he's squealing. That's what they do. What's up with that tree? I'm tryna smoke. Who got it?"

"Holla at Pat. He had it yesterday. See if he got some more." Mousey said.

I went looking for Pat Andrews. I found him in the T.V. room, reading the newspaper.

"Pat, what's up? You got that green?" I asked him.

"Yeah. I got you, but right now, this article in the paper got me fucked up. I can't move from right here."

"What article?"

Pat passed me the newspaper. "Here, check this joint out."

NOTORIOUS D.C. KINGPIN TURNS STATES EVIDENCE ON HIS FRIENDS...

Rayful Edmonds III, was once the most infamous person in Washington D.C. By the age of seventeen, Edmonds III controlled over 90 percent of the cocaine being distributed in the DC area. In 1989 after a lengthy trial, Edmonds III was convicted on the Racketeering Influence Corrupt Organization and Continuing Criminal Enterprise Statutes in a Washington Federal Court. He was sentenced to three consecutive; life without parole sentences and sent to the Bureau of Prison most secured prison in Marion Illinois. Years later he was transferred to Lewisburg Penitentiary in Western Pennsylvania. Edmonds III, from his prison cell in Lewisburg masterminded and orchestrated large scale drug shipments to be delivered to his friends in the District. The suppliers were Colombia Cartel members incarcerated with him at Lewisburg. Edmonds then approached the same FBI officials that ensnared him and alerted them to the drug deals he masterminded. Authorities have arrested 15 D.C. men who were once friends of Edmonds and the Colombians that supplied the drugs. The men arrested have been identified as Tylee Watson, Craig Williams, Adolph Jones, Marcus Hill, Johnny Applewhite, Daryl Smith, Maurice Covington, Lindsey Duvall, Bernard Huff, Clifton Carson, Roy Carson, Michael Johnson, Paul Haleigh, Angelo Hudson, and Xavier Lemen.

I looked up from the paper at Pat. The scowl on his face

was etched like stone. "That faggie ass bitch, moe. I can't believe that nigga did that. He got my peoples all caught up like that. My men was paying my lawyer and all that shit. Now I'ma be fucked up and have to go to trial with a public defender."

"Who's your men? Which one?"

"Tylee Watson. He from my hood."

"I'm sorry to hear that, slim. I'm fucked up myself. That nigga Ray was the most official nigga ever. I grew up hearing about that nigga."

"Bitch made, big lip ass, dick loving nigga. Coward, fuck boy, sucka ass, punk. I wish I could kill that nigga, moe. I'd torture his bitch ass to death. Roast him on an open fire. Rotisserie that rat, moe. Bullshit ain't nothing."

"I feel you, joe. Them rats fuck over good men all the time."

"C'mon, moe. Let's go and smoke. Before I kill somebody in here."

****

My court appointed lawyer came to the jail and told me that there were twelve witnesses in my case. I wondered if my father was one them. I didn't even ask, though. Since we petitioned for a speedy trial, I knew that either I would be judged by one or convicted by twelve. Since I was so young, I was eligible to be sentenced under the youth rehabilitation Act. A youth act would require that after I served an ex amount of time on the Act that my record could be wiped clean. That was probably the best thing for me, I decided.

"Let the government know that I want to cop to a Youth Act." I told my lawyer. No more than 20 years if we can get it."

Two months later, I went to court and copped to Manslaughter and got a 5 to 15- year Youth Act. I turned seventeen shortly thereafter.

"Lorton load…Lorton load…Bracey, Fuller, and Stewart. Bed and baggage. You're going down the county." A C.O. hollered into the day room in the top tier.

"Damn, slim," Mousey said to me, "they sending you down Lorton already. That's crazy."

"Fuck that shit, joe. It is what it is." I replied and went to pack my stuff.

****

Lorton Correctional Complex was about 40 years old and it showed. The bust that I was on drove through the acres of land and I could see a couple different prisons that made up the complex. There were six different prisons at Lorton. The minimum, for dudes that were getting ready to be released in 5 years or less, relatively harmless dudes that couldn't be at the tougher prisons in the complex. The Youth Center One was for dudes like me who had Youth Acts, the Medium, which older convicts called Big Lorton.

There was Occoquan, a maximum security, gladiator spot that everybody called, "The Quack". It was rumored to have landed more medical helicopters to transport stabbing victims than any other prison on the entire East Coast. Then you had Central, a medium security prison that was dubbed "The Hill" because of the hill that it sat on. Lastly, there was the most notorious prison at Lorton and it was where I was headed. All juvenile prisoners had to go to the MAX, nicknamed 'The Wall' and stay locked down until they turned eighteen.

Like the DC jail, we had our own tier. And certainly our

own rules that we played by. The Wall, would either be the death of me or the grooming of a mere seasoned animal. Many people had lost their lives in The Wall and I was determined to not have my name added to that list. Cellblock Two, cell 16 was my assignment and the only person on the juvenile tier that I knew was Black Pug and he had come to Lorton on the bus with me.

The tier at Lorton was different. Dudes had blankets and sheets that covered their cell bars so no one could see who was inside the cells. There was no, 'hey who's in the cell?' or 'Aye main man, where you from?' or none of the shouts that went on when you entered the tier at the jail. On the tier at Lorton, there was nothing but silence. An eerie silence. As a matter of fact, the silence was so loud that it made my stomach do backflips. I moved in and did my cell exactly like all the other cells on the tier.

Later that day, the food trays were passed out by an inmate detail dude. I didn't recognize him and didn't know if he was an adult or a juvenile. When he got to my cell, he didn't even look at me, he just passed a tray through the bars. Then he looked down both ends of the tier and passed me another tray, this one with a cover on it. Confused, I grabbed the second tray and put it on my bed. I uncovered the tray and smiled.

On the tray in the main entrée slot was a fold up street knife, under it was a note. In the two side dish slots of the tray was loose tobacco in one slot and a sandwich bag of light green weed. I quickly grabbed everything off the tray and hid it inside my extra clothes that were new in the footlocker across from my bed. The tray with the food on it was some shit that I barely recognized, a mystery meat of some kind and a green vegetable that I couldn't make out.

The only thing that looked edible was the brown rice. I

moved the food around on the tray and spotted something to the bottom of the rice. Something silver and small. What was on my tray under the rice was a handcuff key. I grabbed it immediately and got paranoid. Who the fuck sent me a handcuff key? I pulled out the note and read it:

Dirty,

What's up, homebody,

Listen, it was a blessing from Allah for me to be able to get over here to Two Block. I'm on another tier though, the adult tier. I heard that you was on the way. My R&D men put me on point. I was in another block, but paid a hefty price to get here arm you and put you on point. If you're reading this kite, you got the Bethleham and the other stuff. Good.

On the other tray is what you'll need the most. Don't ask how I got it, down here them joints are mandatory. You'll need it. On the tier with you is three potential enemies. Dudes ran their mouths and word got back to me that your name was mentioned at a target. I'm not sure what cells they are in, but the Chew Chew from 15th and Death Row is there. You killed one of his men allegedly.

The dude Lil Poo Poo from down the West is there, too. That goes without saying and lastly, the dude Antwan Pringle is on the tier. And he's the dude Ant John's cousin. I wish that I could be down there with you to cook that beef, but I can't. You trained to go, so I feel confident that you'll handle yourself with dignity and honor. I was over the Quack doing my thing until a nigga tried me and I had to bag 'em and tag 'em. That's how I got to The Wall. I'm here to stay until they close this joint.

The detail nigga is a friend. If you need any other assistance, get word to him. With love and respect, loyalty and honor. The Bowlegged One.

Dion. My homie. Dion had looked out for the cookout.

My muthafuckin' man. My heart swelled with Caper pride and manly honor. I flushed the kite and turned the cuff key over in my hand. It was mandatory, huh? Cool. I put both food trays by the cell door and dropped to the floor. I did 500 quick push-ups and then 500 crunches. I had three enemies on the tier and some point they'd strike. Either one or all three. And when they did, I'd be ready. They wanna play? Okay, let's play.

"Aye, Pug? What cell you in, joe?"

"I'm in four cell up the front, moe. What's up?" Pug called back.

"Make a line, slim. I got something for you."

****

The next morning, the CO made an outside rec call. I was up, suited and booted. There was no way that I was going to miss rec. Minutes later, I was handcuffed from the back and told to stand by until a CO could grab me out the cell. I used that time to take my cuffs off. It was easy to do because I'd turned my palms inward instead of outward. Quickly, I slid my knife under my arm and put the cuffs back on.

But instead of putting them on, I rant the connector piece to the side of my cuff. They like they were on, but they wasn't. As the CO's led a line of us to the one big rec cage, I looked behind me and spotted Chew Chew and Poo. I didn't know who Antwan Pringle was. As soon as we made it off the tier and out the block door, I made my move. There were only two CO's escorting about ten of us.

One was in the front and one was at the rear of the line. I slipped the cuffs, grabbed my knife from under my arm and went directly at the first enemy. That was Chew Chew. His eyes opened wide as he tried to brace himself for my strike, but I was too fast, too determined to make an example of one of the three. My first strike was to his body. He shrieked and fell to the ground. Other dudes in the line scattered. I stood over Chew Chew and he kicked his feet out.

I stabbed him in the shoulder and the chest, then his leg and face before I was tackled. My determination and adrenaline had me so zoned out that I hadn't heard a thing. I never heard the CO's call for backup. All I heard was Chew Chew begging for his life.

****

I had heard it somewhere that in war, it was better to take the offensive, than be on the defensive. That's why I did what I did. I know that it was totally unexpected. Nobody thought that I would be prepared for whatever and that was Chew Chew's mistake. He or one of the other two dudes probably wanted to bring me a move once we were all in the rec cage. I was almost sure that, that was the plan.

Well, I spoiled that one and I let the juvenile tier and Lorton know that Dirty Redds had arrived and that I wasn't going for nothing. Chew Chew was rushed to a nearby hospital and couldn't return to the tier when he recovered from my attack. I was put back in my same cell. All I received was an incident report for the attack on Chew Chew. Some privileges that I hadn't even enjoyed yet would be taken, but I didn't care. My mind was on how next to get at Poo Poo and how to identify the Pringle dude.

I wasn't allowed back outside for the next thirty days as punishment for going at Chew. So, I had the opportunity to observe everybody coming and going from rec. My cell was at the end of the tier, but if I stuck a mirror out of the bars, I could see everything and everyone in the front. My next incident happened the third day after I had hit Chew Chew. When it was time to shower, your door popped and you walked down the tier to the shower.

The first time I'd walked down the tier to go to the shower, it had been uneventful. So I figured that whatever would happen next would probably wait until another outside rec situation. I was wrong. On shower day, one person showered at a time for 15 minutes and then went back to his cell. I was coming back from the shower, fully dressed and uncuffed.

I stopped to holla at Pug for a few minutes. He was in the process of sharpening two pieces of steel that we'd exchange with the detail nigga for weed. I saw one of the blankets on the cell that I knew Poo Poo was in move. Suddenly, I felt a sharp pain in my side.

"Aaaarrgggh!" I cried out and jumped back. I grabbed my side.

"Bitch ass nigga stop hollering and drawing a tip. That ain't nothing. I'ma burn your bitch ass up. That's on my mother." Poo spat, then tried to spear me with the knife attached to the broomstick again.

The coward ass nigga had stabbed me in the side with a spear. Once the initial shock wore off and I inspected my wound to see that it wasn't that bad, I laughed. I laughed loud and long. A maniacal laugh, but deep inside I was fuming. "You fuck boy ass nigga…you got that." I walked on to my cell.

I heard another voice say, "You got that bitch nigga, huh, Poo?"

"Yeah, I got him. But I ain't really get him like I wanted too. The banger on the stick shifted. I hit him though, but not like I wanted to. Aye, P, I swear to you, slim, I'ma get that nigga if it's the last thing I do."

I laughed again as I looked at my side. The gash was bleeding a lot and I had no way of knowing how deep it was. I couldn't ask to go to medical because that would alert the cops of the situation and I'd be moved off the tier. Then I'd probably never get back at Poo Poo and catch the dude Pringle.

So, I did what I could. I washed my wound at the sink in my cell and packed a rack of Vaseline on it. Then I ripped one of my bedsheets and a section of my towel. I put the towel over the wound and then tied the bed strip across it until it encircled my waist. I prayed that the bleeding stopped. If it did I was good, if not, I'd bleed to death because there was no way that I was pulling a chicken move like asking for medical assistance.

****

The bleeding did stop, proving that my wound wasn't that bad at all. At breakfast when the trays were passed out, I stopped the detail nigga. "How can I jam this cell door?" I whispered to him. "Up the jail, you can jam the door. Can that be done down here?"

The dude who'd never even told me his name, nodded his head. He gave me a breakfast tray and left. I was confused. Why hadn't he told me how to do it? He'd just nodded and stepped off. At lunch my question was answered. With my lunch tray was a kite and a thin piece of metal. I read the kite:

Take the piece of metal and wedge it between the locking device on the door. You gotta wait until the next time your door opens, though. Your cell door will shut and appear to be locked but it won't. whenever you want to pop out the cell, you just pull real hard on the bars and the door will slide open. This one is on me.

I balled up the kite and flushed it. Then I called down to Pug.

"What's up, joe?"

"Ain't shit, Dirty Redds. What's up with you?"

"Shit. Just tryna read one of them two books you just got. You finished reading either one of 'em?" I asked in code.

"Yeah, moe. I just finished one of 'em. That joint a bad motherfucka hellava plot and all that shit. I gotta order the part two. When you want it?" Pug asked.

"As soon as you can get it to me. I ain't got nothing to read."

"A'ight I got you, fall back."

Pug had just told me that one of the pieces of metal was sharpened and ready for me. I threw my arm back and raised my knee as if I'd just scored a winning homerun.

****

The next evening, Pug came out for shower and ran to my cell...

"Here you go, moe." Pug said and handed me two books. "Read the top one first, it's the best one."

I opened the top book and removed the flat piece of metal that Pug sharpened. It looked just like a street knife. He carved ridges in it and everything. "Thanks, joe. I'ma give 'em back as soon as I finish."

"Take your time. I'm gone to hit this water."

Quickly tossing both books aside, I focused on the metal in my hand. I could actually vision me plunging it into Poo Poo's heart. I took my sheet and ripped it. I used a ripped shred to wrap the blunt end of the metal making a handle for it. Once that was done, I gripped the metal to acclimate myself to my new weapon.

I was ready to work my man. The hot water situation was similar to Oak Hills, where the hot water was in short supply. So what the CO's did was rotate the popping of the cells from front to back to at least let everybody sample some of the hot water. Since Pug was now in the water, I knew that my cell would pop next. Fifteen minutes later, it popped.

"I ain't going to the shower, CO...I'm straight." I stuck my head out the cell and said, all the while jamming the metal into the locking device as instructed. I could hear laughter in the tier from Poo Poo and Pringle, who both thought that I was afraid to walk down the tier past Poo Poo cell.

"Scared ass nigga." I heard Poo Poo say loud enough for the tier to hear.

I smiled to myself and waited patiently to have my laugh. Those who laugh last, laugh best. I tied my shoes up tight and checked my belt to make sure that my pants were secure. My knife was ready and so was I. About an hour after I refused my shower, Poo Poo's cell door opened and he walked out onto the tier.

He was dressed in boxers and Timberland boots, no shirt. A towel was across his neck and in his hand was a shower bag and a change of underwear which I knew had to contain a knife. The fact would have probably made another dude second guess his mission, but not me. Poo Poo had drawn first blood and I was ready to return the favor, regardless of its outcome. But since Poo Poo and I were evenly matched in size and build, I loved my chances to defeat him, even if he was armed.

The beast inside of me told me that I could win. And I always listened to the beast. I pulled the mirror that I used to watch Poo Poo back in. It was time to do my thing. Once I heard the shower water running, I gave it a few minutes to let him get himself wet and soaped up.

Suddenly, it was time to move. Gripping the bars tightly, I summoned my inner Superman strength and pulled the bars completely open. Knife already out, I dashed down the tier. I could hear Pringle shooting to warn Poo Poo, but I kept going. By the time I got to the shower, Poo Poo was picking up his knife.

Naked and wet with soap on his body, he rushed me. His knife was in his right hand. He lunged with and upward thrust. I saw the thrust as an uppercut and threw my left hand down to block it. I shot my right hand out downward and plunged my knife into Poo Poo's chest. He hollered out as he tried to strike again while grabbing me.

"Now look who scared." I muttered while stabbing his shoulder. I had to grab his knife to stop him from hitting me.

"Let my knife go." Poo Poo screamed.

"Shut up, bitch and let me kill you."

We tussled and all kinds of shit, fell, got back up, held each other. I was leaking from a forearm wound. His chest and shoulder was hit. I held his knife hand while he had a death grip on my wrist. I swung my free hand hitting him square in the face, drawing blood.

"You working like a bitch, slim. Let me go so we can push." Poo exulted.

"That's what you want?" I asked him.

"Yeah. Clean break, let's push."

I let Poo Poo's hand go and pushed back real hard until I stood in front of him. We were separated by about two feet. He was hit worse than me and weakening, I could visibly see that. "Let's push." I said to egg Poo Poo. "Let's go." I stepped forward and shot a jab with my left hand, before stepping in with the knife aimed at his face.

He jumped back. He had his boots on, but the soles were wet, making it easy for him to slip. He knew that and I know it. I'd missed my right hand to the face, but connected with a front and a lunge to the body. Poo Poo's knife came down on my left shoulder. I grimaced but ate the pain, he hollered out loudly. That alerted the CO's. They hit the deuces.

"All available to Two Block. All available to Two blocks. Weapons involved."

Poo Poo and I faced off like two bleeding gladiators in a Roman coliseum. I could see the relief in his eyes as the guards ran into the tier and tackled us both. My head hit the ground so hard that I blacked out.

I woke up in the infirmary cuffed to the bed as my fore-arm was being stitched by a doctor. My shirt was gone and a glance to my left showed that my shoulder had already been done. A gauze bandage held by white tape, covered my shoulder wound. Seconds later, a fat black, white shirted, lieutenant approached my bed.

"Fuller, I'm sick of your ass already and you ain't even been here a week. Somehow, you have managed to send two people to the hospital and from what I hear…yeah, I know everything that goes on behind the walls…you're not fin-ished. Well, guess what, you won't get the chance to stab anyone else on my juvenile tier. I wish that I could send your ass to Occoquan or over the Youth Center, but I can't.

Not until the summer of next year when you turn 18. So, until then, you've graduated. I'm putting your ass in a cell on my adult tier, but you'll still shower and rec by yourself. You try any of that pop out your cell shit on my adult tier and I promise you we'll be scraping, what's left of your young ass off the concrete up there. If you think I'm playing; try me." The lieutenant said to me.

To a CO nearby, he said, "After he's finished her, go

ahead and put him upstairs in the first cell. Dead lock it and label it for me."

****

"Young nigga, you a classic." Bowlegged Dion said as he leaned on the bars in front of my cell. "I don't think these people have ever done this before. Putting no juvenile on the adult tier. You done made history at Lorton and you ain't been here that long. Wild muthafucka. So, what's up, dawg?"

"Ain't shit, joe. You know how I get down. Out there, in here. It's whatever with me. Them niggas though they had something sweet. I had to show them that they were wrong. My shoulder hurting like shit, but I'm good other than that. What's with you?"

"For real, ain't no glory in my story. I copped to 15 years on a second degree murder."

"That's the joint you caught on Bladensburg Road?"

"Yeah. Nigga jumped out there and I had to put that dirt over his head. I was over Occoquan, but as usual, niggas think because my eyes are light brown and I'm bowlegged, that I'ma pretty boy. An uptown nigga came in my dorm and broke in my locker. I had them new Washington Wizards Jordan's, some 1300's and a fresh pair of Butters in there. Nigga took my shit, dawg. I couldn't believe it. Word got back to me about who the nigga was. Some nigga from Ledroit Park named Jay. What he didn't know was that I had a brand new Christmas tree.

"Christmas tree?"

"Yeah, that's what my knife looked like. It had ridges on both sides. I called it my Christmas tree. My shit was begging to be tested out on a nigga and Jay signed up to fall on my knife. I went on the other side of the joint on far side and went in his dorm. He had the nerve to be wearing Jordan's when I spotted him. He was laying in his bunk, high as a kite. I butchered his ass. they had to fly that nigga out of here. That's how I got back here. I gotta do a year in The Wall and then I can go back, but from what I hear, that might not happen."

"Why not?" I asked.

"Because we heard that they are getting ready to close this joint. The cops told us that DC ain't paying their bills and these Virginia people that own this land want their land back. So, Lorton is about to close, they said I can believe that too, because they got loads going out all the time. They just sent a rack of niggas to Okie and Red Onion."

"Yeah?"

"Yeah. My man Champ, Buddy Love, Rico Sledge, Gator, Fire, Big Wendell, Michael Howard… all the real niggas done got shipped out. Who else? Dave Battle, Herb Austin, Convict, Donnie Perkins, Zap Out, Bustin' Loose… all them niggas, they gone."

"Your shit lunchin', joe. You naming them niggas like I knew them niggas. I don't know none of them."

"My bad dawg, I'm trippin' thinking you done been down here for a while. Anyway, them niggas are good niggas. You'll come across them somewhere in your travels. But anyway, all of us gon be out in the mountains somewhere or in the feds in a matter of time. So, enjoy your time close to home. Speaking of home, what's up out there? Who you been talkin' to?"

"Shit, nobody really. Just Kemie and Bean. I been so focused on getting at them niggas that I haven't been on the phone, got no package or nothing. I'm surviving off that tree and tobacco you gave me when I first got here. I got a rack of bud in the books though. I just haven't been to the tack.

When I get the phone, I'm only calling Kemie, Bean, and Bay One."

"Bay One? Nigga, Bay One locked up, too."

"What? Stop bullshittin', Dion." I replied incredulously.

"I ain't bullshittin'. They say Bay One killed a muthafucka. She's out Maryland somewhere."

"Wayne Wayne locked up too. He's over Occoquan."

"Wow!" Was all I could say.

"Yeah, and worm is at Maryland, too. His bitch ass out there telling on somebody. I don't know who, though. Dawg, that's fucked up what Creeko and Tee did to Dee."

"I'm hip. That's why they ain't here no more. Shit fucked up out there. Hold on…" I went to my stash and pulled at a stack of pictures. I handed the pictures to Dion. "Here Esha sent me these joints, while I was up the jail."

Dion flipped through the photos. "Damn, look at Esha black ass, phat as shit. You was fuckin' Esha wasn't you, dawg?"

"Naw, joe." I lied. "That's my play sister."

"Yeah, whatever, nigga. I fucked all my play sisters, too. Look at Reesie. Damn, who that is Marnie?" I looked at the pic and nodded. "She ain't Lil' Marnie no more. Damn! Look at Dawn bad red ass. Her and Lil Kesha. This Kemie, dang?"

"Yeah, that's my baby." I replied, not having to see the picture. "All the next 10 or 20 flicks is of Kemie, Reesie, and Reesie's lil sister Tera."

"Who dis?" Dion asked and showed me the picture.

"Oh, that's Kemie's mother, Reesie's mother, and Marnie's mother."

"Damn, dawg. Ms. Brenda and Ms. Tawana can get it. They phat as shit."

"From what I heard they ain't getting high no more."

"Damn."

Me and Dion chopped it up about a lot of other stuff and then he left to go to his cell. I laid down in the bunk and for the first time in a week, I slept good as hell.

****

The rest of my story at Lorton was pretty much uneventful. I got a few visits here and there and pretty much just read a lot. Then a year later, just like Dion had said, they decided to close Lorton. I ended up on a load to Sussex One, in Waverly Virginia. We stayed in Sussex for about a year, then they shipped us to Greenville, in Virginia. We were in Greenville for about seven months before all the D.C. prisoners were shipped to USP Atlanta. The year was 2001 and I was twenty-one years old.

****

"Aye, cuz," My celly, Tiny Crook from California East Coast Crips, called out. "Y' all D.C. niggas care packages came with twelve soaps, a knife and a boy."

I laid on the bottom bunk and laughed until my stomach hurt. "Nigga fuck you, joe. Your homie Baby Yacc told me that you got sexed in on the set."

Tiny Crook laughed. "Shid, cuz, I can't do it like that. I put that work in for the set. Baby Yacc, halfway Mexican ass might've got sexed in, but not me."

"You faking anyway, joe. You ain't never even been to Cochran and Soledad. You ain't been to them real California penitentiaries that my man George Jackson and nem was in. All the real Crips is in them joints. Even big Tookie."

"Cuz, I'm only twenty-three years old. I ain't even been to YA," T.C. said and laughed. "I been to the Crip Module though at the County. That gotta count for something."

"Not with me, cuz, not with me."

I had heard that in the eighties and nineties, DC prisoners and the Crips didn't get along. There'd been all types of wars and bloodshed between the groups. If there was any animosity between the Crips and DC, it didn't exist in Atlanta because some of our closest allies were Crips. So when the bus load came in and Tiny Crook was put in my cell, I didn't trip. I respected men as long as they were men. And T.C. turned out to be a good man. Three years older than me and wild. I loved him. I'd been in Atlanta about three weeks and my fed education was still being learned daily…

****

First I learned the history…

"See, youngin," the old timer Isaac "Flick" Taylor, said as we walked the track on the recreation yard, "Lorton started putting us outta Lorton in the late sixties and early seventies. That's when Lorton was Lorton. What you caught in the 90's was the watered down version of Lorton. Y' all think y' all killing. Youngin' we were choppin' shit up in Lorton.

We used to cut off niggas head and roll one down the walk. We used to stuff bodies in the foot lockers. So, a lot of us got put out of Lorton and sent to the feds. Back in them days wasn't nothing, but six pens and that was this one, Leavenworth, Lewisburg, Lampoc, TerreHarte, and Marion.

They spread us D.C. dudes out into all six. When we came to the feds back then, wasn't nobody black in the feds but big time drug dealers. Wasn't no murderers and robbers and shit. The blacks that were in the pens were getting chumped and punked by crackers, mostly Italians.

When we came, youngin', we changed all of that. You had Native Indians, Colombians, Mexicans, and Whites. We started punking them. Chumping them, robbing 'em and fuckin' 'em."

I laughed. "Y' all was fucking, them dudes, Flick?"

"Youngin', I bullshit with you not. We was some wild young muthafuckas. We was aggressive and playing by no rules. Niggas was fuckin' niggas in Lorton. That wasn't shit.

We didn't care about how we was perceived by others. If you got us wrong, we'd beat your ass, stab you, fuck you, and then kill you. The feds had never seen no black dudes like us. We didn't fear nobody. We came from a 100% black city. We didn't give a fuck about no mafia.

What the fuck they was gonna do? Go in our hoods and kill somebody? They couldn't scare us. We robbed, extorted, beat up, raped, and killed anybody we wanted to. At first it was basically other races. Especially them Natives. They got drunk and loved to fuck.

So we took their reservation money and burned their asses up. Then our cross hairs turned to other blacks. Wasn't no Crips and Bloods back then, Youngin'. Wasn't no GD's and Vicelords, none of that shit. Not in the feds. Well, what happened was, in the late 70's, the white boys got tired of us blacks, robbing, extorting, and fucking their people.

So, they formed the Aryan Brotherhood in the feds. They already had the AB in the California prison system. But they had their hands full with the BGF, Black Gorill Family and the new black street gangs that were rising up on the West Coast. The early 80's was basically the start of the race wars between D.C. and the AB's.

Then at some point they formed an alliance with the Mexicans, the EME, also known as the Mexican Mafia. Back and forth, on both sides, people were killed. We lost a good man named Cadillac in 1982. The homies went beserk. We killed crackers in every joint."

"How long did all that go on?" I asked curiously.

Flick scratched his head. "Probably to the middle of the 80's, yougin' by then we had other problems. Fidel Castro kicked a lot of Cubans out of Cuba. The US Government took 'em in and locked 'em up. That's some foul shit, huh?"

"Yeah."

"Well, that's what they did. Now them Cuban mutha-fuckas was crazy. A lot of 'em were crazier than us. Plus, them Spanish speaking muthafuckas were as black as us. Couldn't tell any of us apart. We warred with them. Then the gangs came. All the ones that I mentioned earlier, that wasn't here.

They started coming in. The Crips, Bloods, Vicelords, GD's, other Mexican gangs, the BGF, the Black P Stones. In the nineties came the influx of the Florida Boys and the Bay Area, the Detroit Boys, and so forth. After 1987 when the crack law came into effect, the feds filled quickly with any and everybody. The Latin Kings came, The Netas, The Black Muslims outta Philly, Jersey, and New York. The Jamaicans came. The Panamanians, Puerto Ricans, Dominicans, Islanders, Asians gangs, everybody.

And over the years, D.C. convicts had warred with every group. We are the only geographical location of blacks on the map that has warred with every RACE, every GANG, and every geographical location and won. Take at least one person from every group, gang, and race and we done either, robbed, extorted, raped, or killed at least one.

No bullshit, Youngin'. God's honest truth. We didn't then and we still don't now, all these years later, give a fuck about nobody, bean eater, gang banger, slant eye, cracka, nobody. That's our legacy, Youngin' and it's up to you and your generation to carry it on."

"No doubt, big homie. I feel you."

"Don't feel me, Youngin. Understand me. When these niggas 'round here heard that busloads of D.C. niggas was coming, man, y' all should've seen all the politicking and meetings. These scared muthafuckas got together and formed all kinds of alliances. Just to combat us, if need be.

The Crips and Bloods went from enemies to friends. They together now. The GD's, Vicelords, P-Stones, Black Disciples, Indians, St. Louis, Kansas City, they are all together. They call it the Midwest Coalition. They whole South, Florida, North Carolina, Virginia, S.C., Georgia, Tennessee, Alabama, Mississippi, about 10 or 11 states have joined together.

They called that the Dirty South. The Latin Kings and the Netas, are swarn street enemies, but in here, they are together. Everybody is together with somebody. All of it done because of you, the homies, because of US. Everybody hates D.C. niggas, but they gotta respect us.

We'll kill them, cops, nurses, doctors, Chaplins, even ourselves. They know that and they fear that. You gotta make 'em continue to fear it, Youngin'."

"I can dig that, Flick, but alotta the homies are in cells with everybody you just named." I informed him. "Including me. I gotta Crip nigga in my cell. And he cool as shit."

"Well, Youngin' it ain't as drastic as I make it sound. It's all true and it's all real, but you got good muthafuckas from everywhere. Just like yo got robbers, killers, extorters, and rapers. We didn't corner the market on that type of shit, we just brought it to the feds and showcased it.

In good times, peaceful times, like now, alotta these out of towners…that's what we call them even though, we are outta town, will be some of the best muthafuckas you will ever meet. A lot of 'em is cool with me. I got white AB buddies, Mexican buddies, Asian, Islander, Cuban, all kinds of muthafuckin' buddies.

I got Crips and Bloods that I love. Vicelords and GD's, all that shit. Some of them muthafuckas I'd die for, Youngin'. I never said that we can't eat off of 'em and eat with 'em, even cell with 'em. I'm just giving you the history of the D.C. blocks in the feds."

"I'ma represent, big homie. But if being a real D.C. nigga means that I gotta fuck with punks and take ass all that wild, geekin' ass shit, then I'ma official Maryland nigga right now." I said jokingly.

"Well, guess what, Youngin'? Start getting your Maryland spiel together." Flick said and laughed. "Just kiddin', Youngin' just kiddin'."

Then I had to learn about the money and hustle…

"Hey Tonie?"

"What's up, Young Dirty Redds?" Antonio "Yo" Jones responded.

"How this money shit go in the feds?" I asked. "I'm tryna gamble and shit and I wanna make sure these bammas ain't getting out on me."

"The money here, Dirty Redds, is stamps. Twenty stamps is a book. A brand new book of stamps at the commissary cost six dollars, right? Well, once it hits the compound, it loses value. It automatically becomes a five-dollar book.

Anything you purchase around here on the compound is gonna be paid in books. You want a haircut, one book. Pair of fifty-dollar shoes, ten books. Ounce of weed, sixty books, etcetera…I was here when the economy of the penitentiary was cigarettes. Then it was picture tickets.

Now food-stamps. You want a soda and a cupcake in the block, that's six stamps. You playing a ticket, you play stamps. You shooting dice, y' all gon' shoot books of stamps. That's the money here in the feds."

Everything else I learned on my own. It wasn't that hard. All I had to do was talk less and listen more. Eventually, I was a seasoned convict, but still twenty years old.

****

"Hey, young brother." A grey haired old man with silver dreads spoke to me.

"What's up, old time?" I replied.

When he walked by, one of the homies, said, "The old timer that just spoke to you is Dr. Mutula Shakur. He's Tupac's father."

"What Tupac?" I asked ignorantly.

"Tupac Shakur. What other Tupac you know?"

"Oh yeah? That's crazy. A nigga in the feds with Tupac's father."

"Good dude, slim. He was a black panther and all that shit. Knowledgeable dude. He be organizing shit in here. Putting shows and shit together."

"Is that right?" I replied.

"Yeah. Holla at him one day. You'll learn something."

A couple days later, I cornered Dr. Shakur in the unit and talked to him. He told me a lot stuff I didn't know.

"Here you go, Youngsta." Dr. Shakur handed me a stack of books. Read these and then come back to me. Will talk then."

In my hand were books by George Jackson, Eldridge Cleaver, Elijah Muhammad, Malcolm X, Che Guevara, Fidel Castro, Arthur Ashe, Muhammad Ali, and Muammar Qaddafi.

****

"What's crackin', cuz?" Tiny Crook asked as he entered the cell.

"Ain't shit, cuz. I'm just reading these books the old timer gave me."

"Let me see what they are." T.C. flipped through the books on the desk. "That's what's up, cuz. I' ma fuck this George Jackson book, Soledad Brothers. I been hearing about it for years but never read it."

"Go, head cuz. I ain't tripping. This nigga Malcolm X was a beast. I'm feeling this nigga." I said and flipped the paper.

****

Two weeks later, I handed all the books back to Dr. Shakur.

"Did you read them all, youngsta?" he asked.

"Every single page of every book." I told him.

"Now, sit in the chair right there and tell me what you learned."

"Well, the one that I liked the most was the one about Muammar Qaddafi.

****

The white boys and Mexicans got into a race riot on the handball court. That put the whole prison on lock down.

"Aye, cuz you ever wonder why we were put here?" I asked my celly.

"Yeah, I was put here because I was robbing banks. I got caught but that…"

"Naw, cuz, I mean on this earth. Why we were put on earth."

"I think I was put here by the Crip God to Crip. Real talk. West Coast Crips!"

"Cuz, you lunchin' like shit." I said and laughed.

Tiny Crook hopped off the top bunk and started crip-walking in the cell. "I'm on the set, cuz. West Coast Crips! Q 102! West Side!"

"Aye, cuz, you might as well do the heehaw. You doing all that jumping around."

"I might not never. West Coast Crips."

"Really, though cuz, I been thinking about my life. About life after death."

"Man, you heard Tupac, cuz, there ain't no heaven for a G. If it is, I'm fucked up then because all my life I ain't wanna do nothing but bang. Just like my big homies. All I ever wanted was to be put on the set. Put in work for the hood. I ain't never prayed to no God, I can't see. Can't hear. Why should I talk to God, cuz, and he don't talk back? Where I'm from in L.A., cuz God don't like gang bangers. Shit is fucked up in my world, cuz. All I knew is poverty, drugs, guns, bitches, and bangin'. Oh and rappin'...you can touch but don't look/you might get hooked/ I'ma brown-skinned crook, holding a blue book. West Coast Crips!"

"See, cuz a nigga can't even have a real conversation with you. You keep acting like you off that sherm."

"I' am off that sherm. That and the pills."

"A'ight. Never mind. I'm good on you right now."

"Naw, cuz, I'm bullshittin'. Go 'head with what you were saying." Tiny Crook said and sat down across from me on the toilet.

"All my life I never though too much about God. I guess I resented him because he let my mother get killed. I don't know. I just know that I never really paid too much, attention to there being a God. Now, don't get it twisted, I feel like you feel about there can't be no heaven for dudes like us. I been killing shit since I was eleven. But my first confirmed kill was when I was thirteen. I crushed both niggas that killed my mother. Months apart. And I knew what the Bible says about killing. But I never really thought about my life, my soul, until now."

"It was them books you read, cuz. You can't be reading that shit."

"I think I needed to read 'em. I like reading 'em. They made me thing. Especially the joints that talked about Islam. I read that Riots joint by Alex Hailey and it said that all the African slaves that came here to America was Muslims.

Look what they did to Kunta Kinte to get him to accept Christianity. Then I read that Malcolm X joint. Whatever is up there, cuz, it changed Malcolm. I believe that. What touched me about that was when he went to Mecca and found out that Muslims were all races.

He prayed with whites, Asians, and a rack of Africans. I think my life been fucked up because I haven't been living right and acknowledging the true Creator."

"And who's that, cuz?" Tiny Crook asked.

"Allah. That's who it is all about, cuz. Allah."

Tiny Crook got up and paced the floor. "I don't know, cuz."

"I'm telling you. If I believe in Allah and submit to him, I think my life will change like Malcolm's did. I'm thinking about becoming Muslim."

"What? Cuz, you might as well become a Crip then. Like you always tell me."

"How you figure that, cuz?" I asked.

"Because, the Muslims are a gang, too. They bangin' and

don't even know it. They structured, they follow laws and rules laid down by a man. Muhammad. We get put on the set and change our names. My name was Vell, short for Arvell, until I got put on.

After I was down with the set, I became Tiny Crook, given that name by the big homie Crook. I'm his Tiny. Feel me? The Muslims do the same thing, but call it something different. They call it taking your shahada. Once you do that, you Muslim, right? A'ight, then they change your name to something else. Abdal, Khalifah, Musa, Ali, or something like that.

Same shit, cuz. Just called something different. If you do something to one Crip in here, you gotta deal with all the Crips in here. Just that simple. Same with the Muslims. You touch one Muslim, they all coming to get a nigga. No questions asked. Same shit. We wear blue and call each other, cuz. They wear beards and kufies and call each other, ock. I'm telling you cuz it's the same shit. You might as well start repping that Cee. We got you, cuz."

"I might not never!" I said and laughed.

****

"Attention on the compound. Attention on the compound. Inmate Luther Fuller report to the visiting room. Luther Fuller! 07650-007, report to the visiting room."

"That'll be you,huh, slim?" Chico asked me.

"Yeah, cuz. That's my baby Kemie. I'ma holla when I get back."

"A'ight, slim. Enjoy your visit."

I walked into the visiting hall and laid eyes on Kemie and I couldn't help but smile. My baby looked good as hell. We embraced and kissed. Her mouth tasted like Jolly Ranchers.

We sat next to each other on couch type seats. "What's up, cuz?"

"Cuz? What the fuck is that? Who is your cousin?" Kemie asked annoyed.

"My bad, baby. My celly is a Crip and that's what they say. He got me saying that shit all the time. But anyway what's good with you? You look spectacular."

"Oh…I do? Well thank you. I take care of myself."

Kemie had on tight jeans, a beige button up blouse opened at the chest to show her cleavage. She rocked a pair of beige and blue Louis Vuitton heels. Her toes were panted red.

"Damn, you look good, baby. I wish I could taste your pussy right now."

"I wish you could too, but you can't so get your mind out the gutter."

Kemie filled me in on everything back home. Then she said, "You been getting all the pictures I been sending you, right?"

"Of course I get 'em."

"I don't want no pictures of me to surface on the internet."

"Don't even trip. As good as you be looking, Playboy will pay us big money."

"Us! Uh, excuse me, brother. They'll pay me big money."

"I thought we were still a team, cuz?"

"We are. I was just playing. I'ma take some pictures while I'm at the hotel down here and send them to you. Reesie flew down her with me. She's at the hotel. After I leave here, we're going shopping on Peachtree. I'ma get her to take a couple naked joints. Can you get those?"

"Send 'em and I'ma get 'em. You bet not have no nigga her with you. Talkin' bout, Reesie came with you. I wanna talk to her later, too."

"That's fine with me. I ain't got no reason to lie to you."

"A'ight. Keep it like that. I love you!"

"I love you, too, boy! Always have. Always will. What you been up to?"

"Nothing much. Going to school. Well, they make you go here. 240 hours. It's cool though, I'ma go head and get my GED. I been working out mostly and reading."

"Reading what? Them, urban novels everybody been talking about lately?"

"Naw. A rack of other shit. I just finished this Ghenghis Clan joint. Some other stuff, too. I'm on a mission to connect with the Creator. Thinking about becoming Muslim."

"Muslim! Boy you don't even believe in God. How you gon' be a damn Muslim?"

"I never told you that I didn't believe in God." I defended myself.

"Naw, you didn't tell me that. But your actions sure did. Ain't no way you could do the shit you do and believe in God. Ain't no way!"

"Well, I do. And I'ma get my life together. For me, for you, for us."

"I hear you, brotha. Preach to me." Kemie said and laughed.

"A'ight you'll see. I'ma come home in a few years a changed man."

"That's good, boo. Because God knows you need to. I'm with you whatever you do. Or don't do. I love you the way you are, but if you change for the better. It's all good."

****

People told me it was a phase I was going through, but I knew better. The more I learned about Islam, the more I liked it. It was totally different from everything else I had learned as a kid growing up. I liked the fact that I could pray directly to God with no middle man. I didn't need to be baptized or stand in front of a lot of people and confess my sins.

I could go straight to Allah with my problems. In the Quran it said that on the day of judgement, God would ask Jesus, "Did you tell people to worship you?" And Jesus would reply and say, "No." My mind would then go to the Bible and I couldn't think of one verse where Jesus told his followers to worship him. In fact, he always instructed the people to worship, him who had sent him.

I learned everything I could about the Moorish Science Temple, the Nation of Islam, and Orthodox Islam, which the Muslims called, Sunnie, because they followed the Sunnah or way of life of the Prophet Muhammad Ilan Adullah, Allah's last messenger and prophet sent to the world. I was turned off by the Meors, because their Circle Seron was the 18 missing years of Jesus life. That gave my spirit no connection to God. I went to the Nation of Islam meeting one day and they had a CD playing.

When the minister Farrakhan said that Elijah Muhammad wasn't dead, that he was on a spaceship that they called the mothership, I ran up outta there. Fast. After alotta thought and reflection, I settled on the Islam that over a billion Muslims around the world practiced. I went to Jumah one Friday and took my shahada. And just like that, I was a different person. Or so I thought.

****

"What's your Muslim name, ock?" Basel asked me one day.

I thought about the book I read on Muammar Qaddafi. I

admired his wisdom and what he stood for in Libya. In two minutes flat, I decided my Muslim name. "It's Khadafi, ock. Like Muammar Qaddafi, but spilled different. I wanna be different. I'ma spell it KHADAFI."

"Okay, ock. All praises due to Allah. Assalaama Alaikum."

I told everybody around me not to call me Dirty Redds no more and that Dirty Redds was dead. I told them to call me Khadafi. It took a while, but pretty soon, everybody called me, Khadafi.

****

"Aye, Khadafi! Khadafi!" somebody tapped my cell door and called out to me.

"Yeah, what's up, cuz?" I replied. I had the towel up covering the window.

"There's a dude that just got here asking people is Dirty Redds on the compound. I don't know the dude or what's up with him. I'm just putting you on point that you're being inquired about. I'm gone. One love."

I knew the voice. It was my homie Nut from Eastgate. "Thanks, cuz." I said back. Getting up off the toilet, I washed my hands and got dressed. I moved the locker back a little and pulled my knife from behind it. I wrapped it quickly and put the handle in it and then headed out the unit. On the rec yard, I saw a group of D.C. dudes. One of the faces I recognized instantly. The other I didn't. I adjusted the knife in my waist. It felt like a gun to me. I paced the crowd and walked straight up to the dude.

"You looking for me, cuz?" I asked him, mean mugging.

"Yeah, nigga." He replied and rushed me.

I grabbed him and hugged him tight. My mean mug

turned into a smile. "Mousey, what's up, cuz? I'm glad that you're here."

"Damn, cuz it seem like you follow me anywhere I go." I told Mousey as I shoveled soaps, tunes, chips, condiments, and hygiene items into a laundry bag. "I can't shake your ass."

"Nigga, you know you love me." Mousey replied.

I grabbed a pair of shoes from under the bed and passed them to Mousey. "Here, cuz, take them blue pumpkin seeds off. These you."

Mousey sat on the bed and put on the white Air Force Ones. "I appreciate this, slim."

"Man, that shit ain't nothing. You my man, cuz. And you solid, so you got all this coming and more. You haven't even seen all the homies, yet. All the good men gon' lookout for you."

"I can dig it. Love is love. How long you been out here in Atlanta?"

"About a year. They sent us out here from Greenville. This spot sweet. You gon' love it, cuz. Where you coming from?" I asked.

"Up the jail." Mousey answered.

"Up the jail? You been up the jail since I left you on the juvenile range?"

"Yeah, slim. I was up there fighting for my life. Shit got hectic."

"What happened, cuz?" I asked and I leaned on the lockers.

Mousey gave me that 'do you really have to ask' look. "You know what happened. Keith happened."

"Get the fuck outta here, cuz. Your codefendant started telling?"

"Did he. Right before trial. The second trial at that. We

gotta hung jury in the first trial. That nigga broke for the second one. Took a cap to like 15 or some shit and gave me up to the people. Lied and everything."

"That's fucked up, cuz. No bullshit. What them people give you for that?"

"Sixty-three years. I'm fucked up in the game, slim." Mousey said, as if resigned to the fact that he was gonna die in jail.

"Bitch as nigga, cuz. I can't believe that nigga did that you like that. After all that shit he don' done in the streets. I used to hear his name ringing out there. He gon' come in and turn bitch. Let them people get him to tell on you to save himself. Bitch made, faggin' ass nigga. Where he at now?"

"I don't know, but I think he Lee County somewhere."

"One thing about the feds is that it's a revolving cycle. All it takes it the right incident to happen here and a lot of us will be shipped outta this joint. He got fifteen years to do. You will never run into because y' all definitely separated from each other. But if I ever run into his ass, cuz. I'ma nail his ass to the pavement. Simple as that. On my mother's grave, you can count on that. What's his name again, cuz?"

"Keith Barnett. Keith muthafuckin' Barnett. Bitch ass nigga."

"I got it, cuz. Keith Barnett. If I ever come across him, he's gonna pay the penalty for his betrayal. Don't even trip. That's my word."

"I believe you, slim. But hey, they got this fat nigga that be with Jay Z named Beanie Sigel…"

"I'm hip to him. Rapping muthafucka." I interjected.

"Well, he got this song called 'What Your Life Like' on his CD. We had the joint over the jail. Anyway, there's a part where slim, says, 'When I get to the fort, fuck a cero pack, gimme the log or a push rod toilet sword.' That's what I'm telling you right now."

I laughed at that. "Oh, my bad cuz. I went to the locker and moved it back. I grabbed my spare knife and gave it to Mousey. "Hey, that dude that came with you, what's his name?"

"Wayne Wayne. Last name Mercer. He's from Lincoln Heights. Why? What's up with him?" Mousey asked.

"Nothing. I just thought I might know him, that's all."

"Still on your bullshit, huh, slim?"

"All the time, cuz. All the time. And one more thing. I don't go by Dirty Redds no more. I got by Khadafi now. I'm a Muslim now."

"Khadafi? That's cool, slim. But you gotta give me a while to get used to that handle. I'm so used to the Dirty Redds joint. I got you, though. And you Muslim, huh?"

"Yeah, cuz. I gotta change my life some."

"If I didn't know you, I wouldn't respect it. But since I beena round you since I was twelve and I know you all man with no cut, I'ma respect that. Most niggas, I hear, be coming to the joint and turning Muslim for protection. But in your case, I know damn well that, that ain't the case. So, I respect that. So, you don't gamble no more? Play cards? Smoke? None of that shit, huh?"

"Nigga, I said, I'm Muslim, not Jesus. Of course. I still do me. I just became Muslim. It's gonna take me a while to cut out all my bad habits."

"Well, in that case, where the smoke at?" Mousey asked excitedly.

"My man Steve Crockett got it. Let's go and find him."

****

On the yard, I saw a lot of the homies huddled up by the

basketball court. My antennas immediately went up. "Something's up with the homies." I told Mousey. "Let's go and see what's up. When we reached the large group of D.C. convicts, I elbowed my way to the front of the gathering. I saw the other dude who had just got off the bus with Mousey standing in the middle with some other dudes. I looked to my left and seen my man Mad Dog. "What's up, cuz? What's going on out here?"

"The new homie Wayne Wayne right here say that Domo is fucked up." Mad Dog told me. "Shorty say that Domo made statements against him back in the day on a body."

"What?" I looked at Dominic "Domo" Gibson and immediately frowned. I never liked that dude anyway. Ever since I heard that him and his codefendant Moe Douglas told on each other. The nigga was a few years older than me and a bit stockier. He was a basketball playing muthafucka and since didn't nobody have no black and white copies of any statements that he made, niggas from D.C. swept the allegations under the rug and made sure that he played for all the D.C. basketball teams in every league. "So, what's up? What's all the pow wousing about? If that nigga hot, let's bust his ass."

"Slim, you know how this fed shit goes. Youngin' ain't got no paperwork to prove that Domo told on him. And nigga fuck with Domo."

Then the dude Domo said something that fucked me up.

"Everybody all out here huddled all up. This shit is too top drawing." Domo boldly stated.

"Ain't nobody do all this shit about Tweet and niggas been saying he hot. Swamp over tier with the Muslims and ain't nobody said shit to him and we know for sure he hot. And that nigga Duke too, why ain't nobody said nothing to them?"

"Nigga," I stepped up and exploded. "Fuck all that shit. This is your second, not first, second call out on some hot shit. If you ain't how, how the fuck your name keep coming up in hot shit?"

"Dirty Redds, you tryna see me or something. I mean you acting…"

"What?" I asked incredulously. Then I snapped. I whipped out my banger and leapt at Domo, hitting him in the neck immediately. He took off running and I had to chase his ass. Over by the bucci ball court, he slipped and fell. I hopped on his ass. Out of nowhere another knife plunged into Domo. I looked up to see; Mousey stabbing Domo. Then a gunshot cracked and stopped our actions.

"All inmates on the yard, get down on the ground or you will be shot!" the recording played in Spanish and then repeated itself. In seconds the entire rec yard was filled with Correctional Staff. Me and Mousey were immediately flexed, cuffed, and picked off the ground. As we walked to the Special Housing Unit, we watched the cops running with Domo on the stretcher pass us, in route to a local hospital, but I hoped it was to the morgue.

****

"Aye, cuz, don't you hate it when rats get aggressive?" I asked Mousey as I made up my bed.

"Slim, I don't even understand that shit. How the fuck a rat nigga gonna act tough?"

I shook my head and sighed. "That's how it is now, though. Every day you hear stories of cold blooded men going against the code and then when they're confronted about it they get on some real live gangsta shit. Rag Baxter, Cornell Thomas, Red Ray from up 640, Ronnie T from the forty, a whole rack of niggas. Too many to count. Niggas is in the streets hanging with rats partying with 'em, hustling for 'em, and killing for 'em. It's sickening, cuz, no bullshit."

I moved over by the shower in the cell to let Mousey make up his bed.

"Damn, slim, I ain't been in this joint 24 hours and I done already caught a stabbing." Mousey said.

"Yeah, my bad, cuz. I wasn't even thinking that you was gonna take off."

"You know I'm trained to go and I know exactly what to do. When you go, I go. That's just the way it goes. I'm cool with that, though. Fuck it. It is what it is. How long you think we gon' be in the box?"

"It depends, cuz. It depends."

"Depends on what?"

"On whether or not that nigga Domo dies."

Knock...Knock...Knock.

I turned to face the cell door and saw a white shorted lieutenant standing there.

"Inmates Luther Fuller and Michael Carter. You both got incident reports. But were sending them to the FBI due to the severity of the incident. If they decide to send them to the US Attorney, then we'll be back to serve you. Okay?"

"Yeah, okay." I replied.

"A'ight." Mousey answered.

Suddenly, Mousey just bust out laughing.

"What's so funny cuz?"

"You nigga. Talkin' bout you changed your life and you Muslim and all that. If what we just did is called changing our lives, I'ma bout to be Muslim, too."

"I told cuz that I still got alotta bad habits and stabbing niggas is one of 'em. I'ma get it together, though. One day. Insha' Allah."

****

"Khadafi?" Mousey called out to me in the middle of the night.

"What's up, cuz?" I responded. I couldn't sleep anyway.

"You ever think about niggas out there fuckin' your girl?"

"Aye, cuz to be honest, I try not to even think about that shit. I don't know, though. Kemie's out there, cuz. I been in here for almost five years. I would be a fool to think that she ain't gave nobody that pussy in all these years. If I think about it too much, it's gon fuck my head up, so I just don't think about it."

"That's the way I used to look at it while I was up the jail. But we had cell phones and shit up there, so I could talk to her all night and during the day. If my bitch was fucking another nigga, she was good because I kept on the phone."

"You kept her on the phone? Why?"

"I was tryna keep that dick outta her." Mousey said. We both laughed at that. "But on some real live shit, being all the way out here in Atlanta and being in the hole like this, it seems like this shit is designed to break your ties with your girl and your family."

"I feel you, cuz. One hundred percent. I been figured that out. That's why I just fall back and do me. I figure that if my aunt Mary, my uncle Marquette, or anybody else in the family wanna holla at me, they know where I'm at. It seem like if I don't holla at them, there won't be no hollering done. I hate feeling like the communication is one sided. Why I gotta always be the one to call or write? Feel me?"

"Hell, yeah."

"My uncle gets at me and sends money all the time. No flicks, no cards, no letters, no nothing. Just money. I can't complain, though. You got niggas in here that people don't send 'em shit. my man Bean gets at me in spats when he ain't locked up. He be flying the flicks in and the money.

He'll hook up with Kemie and they'll send me a rack of shit or he'll pay for Kemie to come down here. My man T.J. is like family to me. He out there but I just found out that somebody done went to his house and killed his whole family. His father, step-mother, and little brother. So, cuz is out there on a warpath.

I gotta few other men out there...Tubby, Pee Wee, Devan, and Fat Rat, but I rarely hear from any of them niggas. But it's cool, though. Like don't stop because one nigga got popped. I just focus on what I can control, cuz that's it. I focus on me and doing time behind these walls. I can't let the street shit keep me side tracked. "Cause then I'm not paying attention to my surroundings.

Atlanta a sweet, joint, it's a rack of money on the pound, but this joint is a sleeper joint. It'll turn deadly in seconds, so you always gotta pay attention to what's right here, right now, in front and around us. If a nigga is fuckin' Kemie, cuz, more power to him. I ain't gon take no dick for her, she gotta take it and that's probably what she's doing right now as we speak. Fuck it, though. That's how life goes. I know that I was fuckin' her probably twice every day.

I know for a fact she had a dick habit when I left. Now somebody else giving her that fix. But, as long as she presses five when I call, fly the flicks in here, write, and send that bread in, how am I gonna complain. And she flies down here, once a month like clockwork. Another nigga got her body, but I got her heart and her brain, so fuck it."

"Everything you just said, slim is some real shit. I be up here in this bunk sucker stroking like shit. Keep picturing Erykah's feet on a nigga's shoulders and shit. Her getting hit from the back or getting her pussy ate. Sucking a nigga's dick. That shit be fucking me up."

"Keep it up, cuz and you lil ass gon' string up. Keep bull-shittin'." I joked.

"Naw, slim. Never dat. I'm stronger than that. I'm just saying, shorty is my lifeline. I don't fuck with nobody else out there. Nobody. But her. So, my thoughts always be with her."

"She know you got 63 years, cuz?"

"Naw. She think I got 10 years. Ain't no way I'ma tell her I'm washed up. I'ma really lose her then. I gotta hold on for as long as I can."

"I feel you, cuz, I feel you."

The Domo didn't die and four months after we stabbed him, the prison let me and Mousey out of the SHU. They shipped Domo to Coleman Pen in Florida. I thought a lot about all the conversations that I had, had with Mousey and other dudes in the SHU. I always come back to the questions that always haunted me. Why was I born? What would the rest of my life be like?

With these questions on my mind I hit the pound running, never quite finding the answers. I continued to study Islam and hang around the Muslims, but I also hung with the D.C. homies and repped my city and hood. I was like a walking contradiction. To me, there were two different sides to me, both fighting for superiority. But together there was a balance.

When the Muslim had problems, I stood with them. When the D.C. homies had problems, I stood with them. But when D.C. and the Muslims clashed, I got out the way. I never let anybody tell that I needed to choose one side. No man could make me do that. My ego and my pride wouldn't allow it. Some days I was the perfect Muslim brother, then other times I was Khadafi the D.C. terrorist.

Both sides coexisted and lived within me. The calm and the beast. Over the next few years, I just settled into my fed bid and dealt with whatever issues that came up. I lost family, friends, and pieces of myself along the way, but I stood strong in my convictions regardless. I went back and forth to the hole for fighting, gambling, and other small shit. But that was just the way it went. Life behind the wall. Then in 2005, Vincent Hill came to Atlanta from Beaumont…

"The dude Vito said something about you killing one of his men back in the day. He's reckless and a loud mouth. You might have to fuck him around." My big homie Chico told me one day. "He's a Wayne Remy flunkie. Other than that, he ain't nobody. You need me to go with you to get him?"

"Naw, cuz. I'm good. Where he sleep at?" I asked.

"He sleep in C building. In C2. On the flats. The 3rd cell coming in the unit, to the left."

"Got it, cuz. I appreciate you. Between you and me, this is probably gon' be my last rodeo. They gon' roll me out for sure after this. You be cool, cuz. One love."

"Same to you, youngboy. One love."

****

"Aye cuz, let me breathe on you, right quick." I told Mousey, pulling him out from in front of the TV.

"What's up, slim?" Mousey asked.

"In the morning, I'm outta here." I told him.

"Outta here, how? Where you going?"

"I gotta bull I need to ride. I'ma do that in the a.m."

"I'm going with you. You know…"

"Cuz, I already know where your loyalty lies. You done proved that a hundred times. But you ain't gotta go on every mission I go on. I been in this spot 5 years. It's time for me to bounce around and see the countryside. My stay in the ATL is over. I haven't heard nothing from Kemie. She ain't been down here in a minute.

What is there for me to stay for? I need a change of scenery, cuz. You, you got Erykah coming through and you eating good. Stay here and do you. You ain't gon' be no good to me from the West Coast. Feel me? You got all my contact info. We go stay in touch. You my man, cuz. I ain't gon' never forget about you.

Even when I bounce in 2008. If I bounce in 2008, you dig? But either way, we connected. If it's meant to be, we'll meet back up. We been doing that since the Receiving Home." I smiled, then reached out and grabbed Mousey. I embraced him. "Death before dishonor, cuz. Always!"

"Death before dishonor. I love you, slim. Make sure you write me."

"I'ma hit Erykah every step of the way."

"Slim, I heard everything you said, and I feel it, but you sure you don't want me to go?"

"I'm positive, cuz. Not this time. Not this time."

****

"Beware of the snake with no rattle and no hiss, it will strike without warning…"

Doctor Mutala Shakur's words crossed my mind as I exited my unit on the first rec move. I walked through the prison with a sense of purpose. I made it to C-building in no time. I slid in the unit as if I had left something and was running back to get it. The cop at the door was a rookie. He didn't know who was in the unit and who wasn't. Good, for me, bad for Vito Hill.

I immediately glanced towards the cell door that Chico had told me Vito slept in. But to my dismay, the cell door was open and the cell light was on. I had hoped, by me coming to the unit so early, that I would catch Vito in the bed. It wasn't meant to be, but I was committed to my task.

I nodded at a few dudes that I knew, who all watched me closely. They knew that I was on something sinister. I had gloves on and a wave cap on my head. My outfit was all khaki browns. At the cell, I peeped in and saw that nobody was inside. So, I looked all over the unit for Vito.

"Where the hell this nigga at?" I muttered to myself.

I checked the showers and the TV rooms. Nothing. I was completely perplexed until one of the homies named Rafael walked over and asked me who I was looking for. I wasn't trying to expose my hand, but I had to. I wanted to get Vito and get it over with. "The big homie Vito. You seen him?"

"Yeah. He in the G.D. nigga Swoll Cell 119."

"A'ight thank you, cuz." I told Raf' and beelined for 119.

I walked past the cell and peeped in the window. Sure enough, there was Vito, standing in the door way talking to the GD dude that was calling shots for the gang on the pound. I didn't want to start a war between the homies and the GD's, but Vito was about to get it in the dude's cell. Hopefully, he's stay out the way. Busting a V turn, I went back to cell 119 and opened the door. Without saying a word, I whipped out and started stabbing Vito in the head and back.

"What the fuck…?"

Vito fell to the ground screaming, "What I do? What I do?"

The GD dude Swoll moved to intervene. I stopping hitting Vito and told him, "This ain't for you, cuz. But you can get some too." To Vito, I said, "Stop all that screaming like a bitch." I hit him as he laid on the floor and kicked his feet out. I had to swat his legs and feet in an attempt to hit him again.

By now a crowd was gathered outside the cell and the CO was in route. I could hear the keys jingle as he ran towards the cell.

"Bitch nigga, be lucky I didn't kill you." I spat at Vito and walked out the cell.

I walked right past the cop who saw all the blood in 119 cell and hit the deuces. My shirt had a little blood on it, but that's it. As the other CO's rushed into the unit, I took off my gloves and handed them and my knife to the homie One Leg Tom. "Get rid of that shit for me." Then I walked to the TV room and sat down.

"Lockdown! Lockdown! All inmates get in your cells! Lockdown!" The lieutenant yelled.

I sat in the TV room by myself watching videos on MTV, until a CO saw me, opened the door and asked, "Lockdown. You gotta go in your cell. Let's go."

"I can't go in my cell." I told him.

"Why not?" he asked.

"Because I sleep in A building. I'm outta bounds."

The CO called out to the lieutenant and told him my story. LT. Stoner knew my M.O. As soon as he saw me he knew the culprit was me.

"Let's go Fuller. You know the drill." LT. Stoner said.

I was taken to the SHU and charged with a 101 serious assault on another inmate. And just like I thought, I never made it back to the compound in Atlanta.

Five months later that, the CO came to my door early one morning and told me I was leaving Atlanta.

"Where am I going, Turner?" I asked.

"Airlift, Fuller. You are outta here." Turner replied.

"Airlift? Airlift to where?"

"I have no clue. I'm just the messenger."

I was put on a bus and driven to the downtown Atlanta airport. A big, white airplane was parked in a vacant lot. Buses and vans surrounded the place. I stood outside and watched as prisoners were unloaded off the plane and then dudes and female prisoners were loaded on. At some point, I was put on the plane. I had never been on an airplane before in my life and I was nervous as hell.

I'd heard all about the feds, raggedy ass airplane and none of the stories ended bad, so I tried to be calm. But when the big white plane taxied to take off, I almost shitted on myself. I closed my eyes and said a silent prayer to Allah. I prayed for a safe flight. Because I was an outlaw and outlaws died the way they lived. Violently, by the gun. Not by plane crash.

After a while the ride became smooth and I eased up a little. I kept my eyes closed and shook my legs the entire time. Hours later, I felt the plane descending. When the wheels finally touched the terrace with a bounce, I could exhale. The plane rode right up to a reddish orange cemented building as if it was an airport terminal.

Minutes later, a CO walked onto the plane. "When I call your name, step to the front of the plane...Dominguez, Morales, Richman, Pitts, Fuller!"

I scooted passed the dudes on my row still sitting down and walked up the aisle of the plane. I stood behind the four other dudes called before me.

"Name and number, Fuller?" the CO asked.

"Luther Fuller, 07650-007." I replied.

"A'ight go 'head off the plane."

I was separated from everybody else, quickly processed into the transit facility and taken to the SHU. "Why am I going to the SHU, CO. I ain't never been here before. Never did anything here."

One of the two CO's escorting me to the SHU, said. "Because you're a really dangerous man, Fuller. At least that what your paperwork says."

"Is that right? Well, do y' all at least know where I'm headed to?"

The CO looked at a paper in his hand. "Says here you're headed to Beaumont. USP Beaumont."

"Not Bloody Beaumont?" the other CO asked.

"Yeah. Bloody Beaumont. And according to this. It's right where Fuller needs to be."

****

"I stayed in Oklahoma for a few days until the bus brought me here. That was over two years ago, cuz. And now you know my life story. Anymore questions?"

"Yeah. What happened with TJ? Did he ever find out who killed his family? Where Bay One and Esha at? And are you still fucking with Kemie?"

"TJ locked up, I heard. Not sure for what. I heard that him and Bean put some work in about his family, but no details really. I know they say TJ shit lunching now, though. Bay One still locked up too. Esha is cool. Last I heard she was still in the hood, doing the same shit. Smoking, drinking, fucking with niggas who got bread. And Kemie, that's still my bitch, cuz. No matter what, she gon always be mine. I talk to her all the time, though. She know a nigga getting short. She tryna claim a nigga again. It's all good, though. I love her dirty ass."

"Damn, slim, you been through some shit. I hope y' all beat that body. If you do, how long you'll have left before you go home?"

"Right, now I got eight months left. Eight months, cuz."

The next morning, I went outside to rec. In the cage were Boo, Umar, Ameen, and me. Umar told us about a conversation that he had with SIS Lieutenant Neal…

"After asking me all them dumb ass questions, he gon' say, "Fuller is scheduled to go home in eight months, Demmer's in ten. Do you think they gon' stand firm on this beef? Somebody is gonna break and they are gonna give you up…"

As we listened to Umar, Ameen paced the rec cage. Then he stopped and said, "Let me tell y' all something. This shit we going through is real. You ain't gon' wake up one day and all this is gone away. They ain't got much, but any prosecutor worth their law degree can paint a picture to a jury using that tape to convict us.

I'm facing the death penalty if we got to trial and lose. By the way, that boy's people been in the papers calling for somebody's head. They'll get mine. Somebody has got to step up and take the beef. They know we were in that room and they got Lil' Cee. Ain't no sense in bullshittin' each other. This shit don't look good for us. We need to make some hard decisions and them now."

"Decisions like what?" I asked confused.

"All three of y' all go home in the next eight to twelve months. If these people indict y' all, y' all stuck like Chuck. I'ma take the beef."

"I can't let you do that, cuz." I told Ameen and meant it. "This is my beef. Keith told on my man, not yours. I killed him, not you. You saying anything right now."

"Naw, scrap. You saying anything. Them people don't know all that stupid shit you just said. I'm already fucked up in the game. I gotta do forty-two years before I see the parole board. I got thirty- five years left before they me give me a five year hit. I'm washed up, scrap. If I cop to the body, all they can do is give me thirty more years at the most. What the fuck is thirty more years when I'll probably die in here anyway? Either way, I'm finished. There ain't no way I'ma let all of us, go down on this body. I need y' all out there on the streets. Who's gonna look for out for all of us as we rot in away in Florence Colorado? Nobody! That's why I'ma take the beef and free y' all!"

I couldn't believe what Ameen was saying. For a second, his face disappeared and I saw Damien in front of me. The sacrifice that Ameen wanted to make was something that Damien would've said and done. Tears formed in my eyes. "You'd really do that for me, cuz?"

"I'd do it for anyone of y' all. But at the moment it's for all of y' all. Y' all gotta be true to the game, respect the code and remember the death before dishonor. And take care of my family. That's all I ask."

Before I knew it, I was crying. My emotions spilled over and like water, from a bucket my tears ran down my face unabated.

Ameen hugged each one of us and said, "I'ma tell Lieutenant Neal that I killed Keith and that y' all didn't have nothing to do with it." He turned to me and said, "You are the first to shine. Make away for Boo and Umar. Then send me some loot and a rack of them internet freak pictures. Then go and hit my daughter's and their mother off. Promise that you're gonna take of my family."

"I promise you that, cuz."

"I love y' all niggas for real. But don't ever cross me." Ameen warned.

"Never that." We all said in unison.

"They gon' put me on a three man hold, so we probably won't rec in the same cages no more. Just keep y' all mouths closed and go home. Do the muthafucka out there for big

Ameen. Insha' Allah, I'll see y' all again, before y' all leave."
Ameen hugged us again. "Aye, CO, can you call and tell LT.
Neal that Antonio Felder would like to see him as soon as
possible? It's important."

Ameen turned back to me and said "Remember scrap,
take care of my family. I guess this is my destiny, huh?"

Before I could say another word, the CO's came and got
Ameen. Once they were gone. I turned to Umar and said,
"That nigga is a real gangsta. I swear on my mother's grave,
when I get outta here, I'ma crush Lil' Cee's mother and baby
sister. Then I'ma find the nigga Eric that told on Ameen and
crush him."

"I feel you, ock. I feel you." Umar replied.

Back in the cell, I told my cell everything that Ameen
said and what he did. "That nigga is the realest nigga in the
world, cuz and I'ma make sure he straight. I'ma hold him
down and show him how other real niggas get down. In eight
months, I'll be home and I'ma catch my first two bodies as
soon as I get off the plane. Watch my work, cuz, watch my
work. I sat on the bed and tears came to my eyes again.

The End

Submission Guideline

Submit the first three chapters of your completed manuscript to ldpsubmissions@gmail.com, subject line: Your book's title. The manuscript must be in a .doc file and sent as an attachment. Document should be in Times New Roman, double spaced and in size 12 font. Also, provide your synopsis and full contact information. If sending multiple submissions, they must each be in a separate email.

Have a story but no way to send it electronically? You can still submit to LDP/Ca$h Presents. Send in the first three chapters, written or typed, of your completed manuscript to:

LDP: Submissions Dept
Po Box 944
Stockbridge, Ga 30281

DO NOT send original manuscript. Must be a duplicate.

Provide your synopsis and a cover letter containing your full contact information.

Thanks for considering LDP and Ca$h Presents.

<u>Coming Soon from Lock Down Publications/Ca$h Presents</u>

BOW DOWN TO MY GANGSTA

By **Ca$h**

TORN BETWEEN TWO

By **Coffee**

THE STREETS STAINED MY SOUL **II**

By **Marcellus Allen**

BLOOD OF A BOSS **VI**

SHADOWS OF THE GAME II

By **Askari**

LOYAL TO THE GAME **IV**

By **T.J. & Jelissa**

A DOPEBOY'S PRAYER **II**

By **Eddie "Wolf" Lee**

IF LOVING YOU IS WRONG… **III**

By **Jelissa**

TRUE SAVAGE **VII**

MIDNIGHT CARTEL III

DOPE BOY MAGIC IV

By **Chris Green**

BLAST FOR ME **III**

A SAVAGE DOPEBOY III

CUTTHROAT MAFIA II

By **Ghost**

A HUSTLER'S DECEIT III

KILL ZONE **II**

Anthony Fields

BAE BELONGS TO ME III
A DOPE BOY'S QUEEN II
By **Aryanna**
CHAINED TO THE STREETS III
By **J-Blunt**
KING OF NEW YORK V
COKE KINGS IV
BORN HEARTLESS IV
By **T.J. Edwards**
GORILLAZ IN THE BAY V
TEARS OF A GANGSTA II
De'Kari
THE STREETS ARE CALLING II
Duquie Wilson
KINGPIN KILLAZ IV
STREET KINGS III
PAID IN BLOOD III
CARTEL KILLAZ IV
DOPE GODS II
Hood Rich
SINS OF A HUSTLA II
ASAD
TRIGGADALE III
Elijah R. Freeman
KINGZ OF THE GAME V
Playa Ray
SLAUGHTER GANG IV

RUTHLESS HEART IV

By Willie Slaughter

THE HEART OF A SAVAGE III

By Jibril Williams

FUK SHYT II

By Blakk Diamond

THE DOPEMAN'S BODYGAURD II

By Tranay Adams

TRAP GOD II

By Troublesome

YAYO III

A SHOOTER'S AMBITION III

By S. Allen

GHOST MOB

Stilloan Robinson

KINGPIN DREAMS II

By Paper Boi Rari

CREAM

By Yolanda Moore

SON OF A DOPE FIEND II

By Renta

FOREVER GANGSTA II

GLOCKS ON SATIN SHEETS II

By Adrian Dulan

LOYALTY AIN'T PROMISED II

By Keith Williams

THE PRICE YOU PAY FOR LOVE II

DOPE GIRL MAGIC II
By Destiny Skai
TOE TAGZ III
By Ah'Million
CONFESSIONS OF A GANGSTA II
By Nicholas Lock
PAID IN KARMA III
By **Meesha**
I'M NOTHING WITHOUT HIS LOVE II
By Monet Dragun
CAUGHT UP IN THE LIFE II
By Robert Baptiste
NEW TO THE GAME III
By **Malik D. Rice**
LIFE OF A SAVAGE III
By **Romell Tukes**
QUIET MONEY II
By **Trai'Quan**
THE STREETS MADE ME II
By **Larry D. Wright**
THE ULTIMATE SACRIFICE VI
By **Anthony Fields**
THE LIFE OF A HOOD STAR
By Ca$h & Rashia Wilson

Available Now

RESTRAINING ORDER **I & II**
By **CA$H & Coffee**
LOVE KNOWS NO BOUNDARIES **I II & III**
By **Coffee**
RAISED AS A GOON I, II,   III & IV
BRED BY THE SLUMS I, II, III
BLAST FOR ME I & II
ROTTEN TO THE CORE I II III
A BRONX TALE I, II, III
DUFFEL BAG CARTEL I II III IV
HEARTLESS GOON I II III IV
A SAVAGE DOPEBOY I II
HEARTLESS GOON I II III
DRUG LORDS I II III
CUTTHROAT MAFIA
By **Ghost**
LAY IT DOWN **I & II**
LAST OF A DYING BREED
BLOOD STAINS OF A SHOTTA I & II III
By **Jamaica**
LOYAL TO THE GAME I II III
LIFE OF SIN I, II III
By **TJ & Jelissa**
BLOODY COMMAS I & II
SKI MASK CARTEL I   II & III

Anthony Fields

KING OF NEW YORK I II,III IV

RISE TO POWER I II III

COKE KINGS I II III

BORN HEARTLESS I II III

By **T.J. Edwards**

IF LOVING HIM IS WRONG...I & II

LOVE ME EVEN WHEN IT HURTS I II III

By **Jelissa**

WHEN THE STREETS CLAP BACK I & II III

THE HEART OF A SAVAGE I II

By **Jibril Williams**

A DISTINGUISHED THUG STOLE MY HEART I II & III

LOVE SHOULDN'T HURT I II III IV

RENEGADE BOYS I II III IV

PAID IN KARMA I II

By **Meesha**

A GANGSTER'S CODE I &, II III

A GANGSTER'S SYN I II III

THE SAVAGE LIFE I II III

CHAINED TO THE STREETS I II

By **J-Blunt**

PUSH IT TO THE LIMIT

By **Bre' Hayes**

BLOOD OF A BOSS **I, II, III,   IV, V**

SHADOWS OF THE GAME

By **Askari**

THE STREETS BLEED MURDER **I, II & III**

Khadafi

THE HEART OF A GANGSTA I II& III

By **Jerry Jackson**

CUM FOR ME I II III IV V

An **LDP Erotica Collaboration**

BRIDE OF A HUSTLA **I   II & II**

THE FETTI GIRLS **I, II& III**

CORRUPTED BY A GANGSTA I, II III, IV

BLINDED BY HIS LOVE

THE PRICE YOU PAY FOR LOVE

DOPE GIRL MAGIC

By **Destiny Skai**

WHEN A GOOD GIRL GOES BAD

By **Adrienne**

THE COST OF LOYALTY I II III

By Kweli

A GANGSTER'S REVENGE **I II III & IV**

THE BOSS MAN'S DAUGHTERS I II III IV V

A SAVAGE LOVE   **I & II**

BAE BELONGS TO ME I II

A HUSTLER'S DECEIT I, II, III

WHAT BAD BITCHES DO I, II, III

SOUL OF A MONSTER I II III

KILL ZONE

A DOPE BOY'S QUEEN

By **Aryanna**

A KINGPIN'S AMBITON

A KINGPIN'S AMBITION **II**

I MURDER FOR THE DOUGH

By **Ambitious**

TRUE SAVAGE I II III IV V VI

DOPE BOY MAGIC I, II, III

MIDNIGHT CARTEL I II

By **Chris Green**

A DOPEBOY'S PRAYER

By **Eddie "Wolf" Lee**

THE KING CARTEL **I, II & III**

By **Frank Gresham**

THESE NIGGAS AIN'T LOYAL **I, II & III**

By **Nikki Tee**

GANGSTA SHYT **I II &III**

By **CATO**

THE ULTIMATE BETRAYAL

By **Phoenix**

BOSS'N UP **I , II & III**

By **Royal Nicole**

I LOVE YOU TO DEATH

By Destiny J

I RIDE FOR MY HITTA

I STILL RIDE FOR MY HITTA

By **Misty Holt**

LOVE & CHASIN' PAPER

By **Qay Crockett**

TO DIE IN VAIN

SINS OF A HUSTLA

Khadafi

By **ASAD**

BROOKLYN HUSTLAZ

By **Boogsy Morina**

BROOKLYN ON LOCK I & II

By **Sonovia**

GANGSTA CITY

By **Teddy Duke**

A DRUG KING AND HIS DIAMOND I & II III

A DOPEMAN'S RICHES

HER MAN, MINE'S TOO I, II

CASH MONEY HO'S

By Nicole Goosby

TRAPHOUSE KING **I II & III**

KINGPIN KILLAZ I II III

STREET KINGS I II

PAID IN BLOOD **I II**

CARTEL KILLAZ I II III

DOPE GODS

By **Hood Rich**

LIPSTICK KILLAH **I, II, III**

CRIME OF PASSION I II & III

By **Mimi**

STEADY MOBBN' **I, II, III**

THE STREETS STAINED MY SOUL

By **Marcellus Allen**

WHO SHOT YA **I, II, III**

SON OF A DOPE FIEND

Anthony Fields

Renta

GORILLAZ IN THE BAY **I II III IV**

TEARS OF A GANGSTA

DE'KARI

TRIGGADALE I II

Elijah R. Freeman

GOD BLESS THE TRAPPERS I, II, III

THESE SCANDALOUS STREETS I, II, III

FEAR MY GANGSTA I, II, III

THESE STREETS DON'T LOVE NOBODY I, II

BURY ME A G I, II, III, IV, V

A GANGSTA'S EMPIRE I, II, III, IV

THE DOPEMAN'S BODYGAURD

Tranay Adams

THE STREETS ARE CALLING

Duquie Wilson

MARRIED TO A BOSS... I II III

By Destiny Skai & Chris Green

KINGZ OF THE GAME I   II III IV

Playa Ray

SLAUGHTER GANG I II III

RUTHLESS HEART I II III

By Willie Slaughter

FUK SHYT

By Blakk Diamond

DON'T F#CK WITH MY HEART I II

By Linnea

Khadafi

By **Trai'Quan**

THE STREETS MADE ME

By **Larry D. Wright**

THE ULTIMATE SACRIFICE I, II, III, IV, V

KHADIFI

By **Anthony Fields**

THE LIFE OF A HOOD STAR

By **Ca$h & Rashia Wilson**

Khadafi

BOOKS BY LDP'S CEO, CA$H

TRUST IN NO MAN

TRUST IN NO MAN 2

TRUST IN NO MAN 3

BONDED BY BLOOD

SHORTY GOT A THUG

THUGS CRY

THUGS CRY 2

THUGS CRY 3

TRUST NO BITCH

TRUST NO BITCH 2

TRUST NO BITCH 3

TIL MY CASKET DROPS

RESTRAINING ORDER

RESTRAINING ORDER 2

IN LOVE WITH A CONVICT

LIFE OF A HOOD STAR

Coming Soon

BONDED BY BLOOD 2

BOW DOWN TO MY GANGSTA

CPSIA information can be obtained
at www.ICGtesting.com
Printed in the USA
LVHW010704070621
689548LV00008B/501

9 781952 936081